DEFENSE OF THE NEST

DEFENSE OF THE NEST

DRAGON APPROVED™ BOOK THREE

RAMY VANCE

MICHAEL ANDERLE

DISRUPTIVE IMAGINATION

THE DEFENSE OF THE NEST TEAM

Thanks to the Beta Readers
John Ashmore, Kelly O'Donnell

Thanks to the JIT Readers

Kathleen Fettig
Dorothy Lloyd
Misty Roa
Diane L. Smith
Deb Mader
Jeff Goode
Larry Omans
Jeff Eaton

If I've missed anyone, please let me know!

Editor
The Skyhunter Editing Team

LMBPN Publishing
PMB 196, 2540 South Maryland Pkwy
Las Vegas, NV 89109

First US Edition, January 2020
Version 1.01, February 2021
eBook ISBN: 978-1-64202-706-8
Paperback ISBN: 978-1-64202-805-8

DEDICATION

To Brett Dillion Barr ... and his Stewing influences...

—Ramy Vance

*To Family, Friends and
Those Who Love
to Read.
May We All Enjoy Grace
to Live the Life We Are
Called.*

— Michael

CHAPTER ONE

Alex woke in a room that felt strange. She hesitated to open her eyes.

The darkness was home.

It was closer than family; it was life. No matter how far she got away from it, the darkness was always there. It was part of her in some way, maybe more a part of her than she would care to admit.

She remembered vividly the last thing she'd seen. She almost laughed. "Seen" was a word she had never thought she would have a use for, yet it was what she had *seen* that had sent her screaming.

It hadn't been anything specific. Nothing had jumped out or scared her or anything like that. She had just seen—truly *seen* for the first time. There had been different iterations of what sight could be like for her: *Middang3ard VR*, the vision provided by Myrddin, and Manny's multiple eyes.

There was something else too. Her own eyes were working now. Well, not fully. Whatever Myrddin had done had brought her sight, sort of, but it was overwhelming.

Adjusting to her new ability would take longer than getting used to seeing through Chine's or Manny's eyes had.

And it hurt to look through her own eyes. It hurt so much that she never wanted to open her eyes again.

As in, *ever*.

Even with her eyes closed, Alex knew someone else was in the room. She could hear their breathing. Thankfully, Alex could also feel fabric wrapped around her eyes. Someone'd had the decency to blindfold her, which meant she didn't need to let anyone know she was awake.

Whoever was in the room wasn't worried about talking or checking on Alex, which was great. She needed time to get her thoughts together. Life kept coming at her, harder every time. Being able to see was supposed to be the easy part of joining the dragonriders.

Alex tried to think back to what had happened. She tried to paint the picture in her mind, but she was unfamiliar with the task. Recalling images from in-game was one thing, but the real deal, trying to remember what *she'd* seen, felt a thousand times harder.

It could be done, though. Since Alex had arrived at the Wasp's Nest, she'd been filled with the feeling that she wasn't good enough, that she wasn't going to be able to complete whatever task was set before her. She had to get over that and soon.

She could start by remembering.

The last image Alex recalled came at her, surrounded by a headache. Even trying to piece together memories visually was enough to make her want to grab her head and scream, but she needed to do this.

What kind of dragonrider was she going to be if she couldn't even do this one thing?

Alex took a deep breath and hoped whoever was in the room wasn't paying attention enough to notice. The last thing she could remember was seeing her own eyes through Chine's , dissecting her own pores, and noting her own hair follicles.

True sight hadn't knocked Alex on her ass. It had been Chine's sight that was too much to handle. She was seeing something beyond what human beings saw.

How was that any different than when she was looking through Manny's eyes, though? He didn't see the same way humans did. When Manny explained it to Alex, he'd mentioned seeing on entirely different planes of existence.

Yet Manny's vision seemed dull in ways that made *Middang3ard VR* seem vibrant.

Alex could not see it, but she was lying in a bed in Sickbay. For most of the afternoon, she'd been attended to by a host of nurses and doctors trying to figure out what was wrong.

On the surface, it didn't seem like anything. Her eyes were still technically dead, but that was to be expected since Myrddin couldn't have cast a successful healing spell on something that was not injured. So, the doctors continued to look.

Manny had the most reasonable explanation. Alex had been asleep while Manny'd tried to explain to the doctors what he thought was happening.

Needless to say, the doctors didn't listen. Manny was, in fact, merely Myrddin's messenger. What would he know of these things?

After the doctors left, Manny stayed behind. The breathing Alex had heard when she woke up belonged to him. He'd stayed with her through the first and second day she'd been in the hospital. Not a moment had passed without him at her side.

Alex would never know that, though. Manny had no intention of telling her; he didn't think it was necessary. He knew someone had to watch over the girl, and he was the most likely candidate.

The door to Sickbay creaked as it opened. Alex tried not to shift or show any sign she was awake. She didn't want to deal with anyone. Unless they could tell her how she could see comfortably, it wasn't of any concern to her. She'd rather lie in the dark and think.

She heard Myrddin's voice; it was soft, perhaps concerned, but she couldn't read the intention behind his words. Having now seen his face while he'd spoken made interpreting even harder. Alex had the feeling Myrddin was not a man you could understand, not unless he wanted you to.

Myrddin sounded as if he were speaking underwater. There was the vague recollection of a sound, but nothing actually there; it must have been magic. Alex assumed it was the only way he'd be able to do such a thing.

Manny, on the other hand, could be heard loud and clear. "She's been sleeping for a while. I think we should let her rest."

Myrddin spoke again, but it was impossible to hear. Alex almost considered sitting up just so she could ask Myrddin to stop the magic nonsense to let her hear what they were talking about. If secrecy was so important, Myrddin and Manny could take the conversation outside.

Manny's voice cut through Alex's internal monologue. "I know you don't think it's important, but she needs to rest," Manny argued. "If you push her further, there may not be any coming back. This might be it. And will you please get rid of that muffled effect? I can hardly hear what you're saying."

There was a suspiciously loud cough before Alex heard a

noise as if someone had just popped a bubble with a needle. Myrddin's voice came through clear as the crystal palace surrounding them. "Time is running out," he hissed. "What is wrong with her?"

Manny gave a huge sigh, and Alex had to squash the desire to get up, rip off her blindfold, and glare at them both. "She isn't able to see through the dragon eyes yet," Manny explained. "She hasn't ever seen—really seen, and this? This is something completely new for her system to deal with. You're expecting a lot from her."

"We all expect a lot from her. Whether it is just me or a collective force doesn't matter. She is a necessary member of the dragonriders now. I do not—"

"If she is necessary, then you should make an effort to understand. She's been seeing mostly through my eyes. It's different from VR. Beholders see multiple levels of reality at the same time, and we filter it automatically. Everything Alex has seen through my eyes has been unconsciously tempered so it doesn't fry her brain. What you did with the dragon's eyes pushed the boundaries."

Alex stopped herself from grabbing her sheets as she held her breath. "What you did was dangerous, Myrddin," Manny chastised. "You could have shattered her mind, giving her the sight of a dragon. What were you thinking?"

Alex heard Myrddin cross the room, his robes chafing against his thighs. "I did what I had to do," he replied. "She needs to see. I gave her the best sight imaginable—to see through the eyes of a dragon. Even you would be envious of such a thing."

"And because of that, I would know not to bestow dragon sight upon a child who has never used her eyes before."

"I do not have time for this," Myrddin spat. "Nor do any of the realms. You will stay with her during her training. Be her eyes if she cannot deal with the eyes of the dragon. We have to get these recruits ready for what is coming. We have..."

Myrddin's voice trailed off. Alex could imagine him stroking his beard as he looked for the right words to say. She didn't think he would find them.

Her heart was racing. Myrddin had spoken about her as if she were some tool—necessary and with value, but almost lacking in humanity. *What the hell have I gotten myself into?* she thought.

Manny coughed nervously before he replied to Myrddin. "Fine," he finally said. "I'll stay with her and help as much as I can. But you must realize what you're doing and the strain you are placing on this girl."

Myrddin opened the door. "I am completely aware of what I am asking," he retorted. "If she is not able to perform, then I made a mistake in choosing her, nothing more and nothing less. Provide her the assistance she needs. The training continues. If she keeps up, she keeps up. If she fails, we'll figure it out from there."

The door clicked. Alex assumed Myrddin had left Manny alone in the room with her. There was no way to know whether Manny knew she was awake, but she figured it didn't matter either way.

The way Myrddin had talked about her had filled the dragonrider with rage. Alex wished she had spoken up, but she had no idea what she would have said. Regardless of how single-minded Myrddin was being, he was right. If she couldn't keep up, she should do something else.

Alex wanted to go back to sleep. She felt like her insides were trying to twist away from her. Maybe she didn't belong here. *Middang3ard VR* could have been an extended fluke. The real thing, the real and true war of Middang3ard, might be too much for her to handle.

The fear that hit Alex was not something she'd ever experienced before. It started at her throat and she seized up, gasping for air. Then it traveled down her chest, and her lungs grew tight as if she would never breathe again.

Finally, it pooled in her stomach. Her guts constricted with cramps she'd never felt before. She wanted to scream. The pain was nearly as bad as looking through Chine's eyes for the first time. *I'm not going to be able to do this*, Alex thought. *I can't do this.*

As Alex descended into a pit of self-doubt, she tried to think of something to encourage herself, but there was nothing. All of the kind words her parents had shared with her had disappeared. It was like they'd never been said. The darkness was looming—the true darkness.

Manny burped softly in the corner of the med-bay. "Excuse me," he muttered.

His decorum made Alex want to laugh, but she held it in. She didn't want him to know she'd been even slightly awake for his and Myrddin's conversation.

At least Manny was here. He apparently didn't begrudge Alex anything. In fact, he seemed more on Alex's side than Myrddin did. Manny hadn't forgotten Alex was a person, not just a thing to be used as Myrddin saw fit.

She stretched her arms and her legs, making a big show of waking up. After she sat and yawned dramatically, she asked, "Where am I?" in a feigned sleepy voice.

When Manny spoke, he sounded much closer to Alex than when he'd been talking with Myrddin. "Oh, thank the gods you're awake," he exclaimed. "You've been out forever. Are you feeling better?"

"Yeah, a little bit. Hey, Manny, can I ask you a favor?"

"Sure, whatever you need."

"Could you...help me see? Whatever spell Myrddin cast was too strong. Could I use your eyes again—just until I get used to everything?"

He didn't bother answering, but Alex felt the warmth behind her eyes. She thought this was the best way to take some of the pressure off Manny. Hopefully, if it seemed like her idea, he wouldn't be too stressed. "Thanks, Manny."

She pulled the blindfold up on one of her eyes so she could look at Manny. He floated in front of her, a bright green color, with his tendrils nervously waving back and forth as his largest eye stared at her with hope and worry. "We've got to get you rested up. Training starts soon."

"Will you help me with my training?" Alex asked as she pulled the blindfold down again. Her eyes still weren't quite there, and it was easier to not use them—for now, at least.

She could hear the smile and genuine enthusiasm in his voice when he replied, "I'd love to."

"All right, that sounds good. But I need to rest, Manny. Do you think I could be alone for a while? Just by myself."

"Oh, yes, of course. Not a problem."

Manny spoke again as he moved toward the door. "Just one thing," he started. "You'll be moved into your dorm room during the night. I just didn't want you to wake up and be scared."

Having Manny put forth an effort to make her comfortable warmed Alex's heart. She felt like there was at least one person here rooting for her. "Thanks for the heads up, Manny. I really appreciate it."

"No problem." There was the same click of the door and Alex was alone.

Not once in her entire life had there been anything Alex didn't think she was capable of. Now, in Middang3ard, Alex was struck with the overwhelming idea that being a dragonrider was something she might not be able to do.

It wasn't enough to believe in herself. She'd believed in herself her entire life. This was something new. She couldn't quite get her head around it. She kept repeating to herself that she could do this, but every time she said the words, they became hollower.

What if this is not *something I can do?*

The thought was too much for Alex to bear. She succumbed to a darkness more familiar than that which was growing and taking on a life of its own. Sleep came upon her quickly, and soon after, she was in her dreams, which had never taken on a specific form.

CHAPTER TWO

Alex was jolted awake by a nightmare. She couldn't control her breathing. Her heart was pounding in her chest, and she instinctively leaped from her bed, only to crumple to the crystal floor as she tried to figure out where she was.

The blindfold had fallen off her face. She fumbled around on the floor looking for it before deciding she didn't need it. Still, she picked it up and felt around a little bit more to understand where she was in relation to the rest of the room.

Once Alex touched the bed, she grabbed the posts and pulled herself closer to its comfort. She sat down and tried to steady her breath and keep her eyes from opening. Even though she'd never been able to see before, she could always feel light on the back of her eyelids.

That light was what called her to open her eyes. It was like a question waiting to be answered.

Suddenly, Alex remembered what Manny had told her— she was going to be moved to her dorm room during the night. Everything felt foreign because she wasn't in the med bay anymore. This was a new place, nothing else.

Alex listened to see if there was anyone in the room with her, but she couldn't hear any moving or breathing. *I must be alone,* she thought thankfully. *Now is as good a time to try and figure this crap out.*

Just to be safe, she refolded her blindfold.

Inhale. Exhale. Inhale and hold it. Alex ran through the exercises she'd been taught to handle her anxiety in new situations before she cracked her lids open.

The light in the room hit her eyes and went straight to the back of her head. She felt dizzy, and like she might throw up. She pitched forward, clutching her gut and closing her eyes as tightly as she could until the pain passed.

When she took another deep breath and tried to open her eyes, she couldn't. There was no way to get past the light, which was otherworldly-bright. She pulled her knees close and cried softly from the pulsing awakening in her head as she put the blindfold back on.

The sound of the door opening broke her reflections, and she jumped. "Who's there?" Alex asked, her voice cracking.

The sound of beating wings filled the room, and they were getting closer. "It's me, Jollies. Just got back from breakfast. Figured you didn't have any. Hold on, all right?"

Jollies' fluttering wings disappeared for a moment, came back, then vanished again. The noise continued for a couple of minutes until the door shut completely. Alex felt a tiny soft hand on her wrist. The touch moved down her hand to her finger, grabbing it tightly.

Jollies guided Alex to the desk by tugging on her finger. There were two plates of food there that Alex hadn't even smelled because Jollies had been moving so fast.

She moved Alex's hand to a pair of utensils and released her. "Got the best of the best. Don't want you going hungry or anything like that."

Alex dug into the food. She was famished. The night of

11

sleep had been good for her head but not her stomach. She ate so fast that she hardly tasted what went into her mouth. She was too busy inhaling everything edible near her. Suddenly she stopped. "Wait, how did you get all this here?"

Jollies laughed, and Alex could hear her zipping around her head. "Pixies are extremely strong. We can lift nearly three hundred times our body weight. You can't tell when you look at me, but..."

Jollies' voice trailed off. Alex was used to that happening. A lot of people thought she would be offended at the choice of words, but Alex had come to terms with that a long time ago. It was just a phrase.

Alex smiled to let Jollies know everything was okay. "Don't worry about it. I know what you mean," Alex said. "And when I did see you, I wouldn't have imagined you could lift so much."

"Yeah, I could probably lift you if I put my mind to it."

Alex burped loudly as she wondered if she could cram any more food into her stomach. "So, what all did I miss?" Alex asked. "I'm assuming Gill and Brath had something to say about me passing out."

Jollies didn't answer at first. Alex wished Manny was there. She'd started to get used to looking at new people as she spoke. Finally, Jollies answered, "Well, Gill didn't say much," Jollies admitted. "But Brath...he had a lot to say. It's probably best if I leave it to your imagination."

"You know, usually, it's the opposite of that. You don't leave it up to anyone's imagination because they make it worse than what was actually said."

"Oh, well. He said you're a pathetic human who will never amount to anything in the dragonriders, and it would have been better for you if you'd never been born."

Alex sat there quietly for a moment while she tried to compose herself. She remembered what Jollies had told her about Brath, about him losing his home realm. That didn't make his words sting any less. "Maybe I should have just used my imagination." Alex groaned.

"You gonna tell me what Myrddin did to you that made you pass out?"

Alex pointed to the blindfold around her eyes. "Well, no reason to beat around the bush," she said. "Everyone knows I'm blind. Myrddin cast a spell that gave me sight, but it turns out he gave me dragon sight, and it's tied to Chine. It's too detailed and too focused, especially for me."

"Maybe you just need practice."

Jollies flew over to Alex and landed on her shoulder. "What if I helped you get a handle on all this?" the pixie asked. "I mean, we *are* roommates and everything. We're going to be spending a lot of time together. It's probably like using a muscle."

Alex tilted her head in the direction of Jollies' voice. "What do you mean?"

"You know how if you don't use a muscle for a long time, it gets weak? Since you've never really used your eyes, you're probably not used to flexing that muscle. It might just take practice. Like, we should train you up to it?"

"Sounds like bad anime."

"That's one of those human cartoons, right?"

Alex chuckled as she nodded her head. "Do you know anything about humans? Like, our culture or anything?"

"Probably about the same amount you know about pixies. Things I've read or was told about. You're the first human I've ever met, not counting Myrddin. I personally don't think he's human anymore, though. Now, you ready to give it a try?"

Alex sighed. She didn't want to look weak in front of Jollies. Asking for help was not something she was particularly good at; it rubbed her the wrong way. But Jollies was offering to give her a hand, and it was fairly obvious she needed the help. "All right," Alex muttered.

"Great!" Jollies exclaimed as she flew around Alex's head. "We should start with something small. Like, I will pick something, and you see if you can look at it. How's that sound?"

It sounded like Jollies was pulling ideas out of her ass, but that didn't keep her mood from being infectious. "All right. What are we going to start with?" Alex asked.

Jollies grabbed Alex's hand again and pulled it across the table, resting it on what felt like a clock. Alex felt around until she was certain. "The clock?"

"Exactly. I figured that would be easy enough. Now, take off your blindfold, and let's get started."

Alex removed the blindfold and held it in her palm. Her eyes were still shut tightly. She was afraid of opening them. The pain was going to come instantly, just as it had before. She wanted to avoid the pain—and to avoid the failure.

Jollies tapped Alex's ear impatiently. "Ready?" she chirped.

I'm going to have to figure this out sometime, Alex thought. *Otherwise, I can kiss riding Chine goodbye.*

The thought of riding the dragon perked Alex up. There had been so much going on that she'd briefly forgotten she was enrolled in a program that would take her back to the skies. She couldn't give up yet. There was no way she was going to let that possibility slip away.

Alex peeked through her left eye, opening it a crack—hardly at all. The pain was immediate. The light in the room was like a knife to her eye socket. She yelped with pain and shut it before the headache could set in.

Jollies flew down and rested on Alex's hand. "You hardly even got one open!"

"Jollies, I know that. It's a lot harder than it seems."

"I'll say. It looks like you're having a *very* hard time."

"I don't know what pixies think is encouraging, but by human standards, you're terrible at it."

"Pixies don't encourage. We motivate. Now get those eyes open! You wanna fly, don't you?"

Alex felt like Jollies had read her mind, but in all honesty, it wouldn't have taken too long to figure out. They all were here for the same thing, except maybe Jollies since she could already fly. "All right, I'll try again," Alex grumbled.

She pulled down her blindfold again. This time she opened her right eye less than before, and the light felt less aggressive. It still felt searing in its intensity, but more manageable.

Next, she opened her eye a little more, almost as wide as she'd opened it earlier. Now the light was flowing in, and everything was too white and hot. She had to stop. It hurt too much.

Jollies' voice rang sharply in Alex's ear. "There you go!" the pixie squeaked. "It's more open than before! You're almost there. Just take a deep breath. Concentrate and you'll get there."

Alex snapped her eye open. She didn't want to waste half an hour on this. Her vision blurred as intense color overloaded her brain, but she looked straight ahead and reached out for the clock she knew was in front of her.

Slowly, the clock started to take shape, the colors distinguishing themselves from each other, like the sharp blackness of the clock's hands. Then the excruciating details became clear. Alex winced as her eyes picked up the specks of dust on the clock's face.

Now would have been a great time to take a break, but Alex felt she'd accomplished so much already. Her eye was open. She had to see how far she could take it.

Slowly, she opened her other eye. It was the same thing.

At first, it was too much to handle, but the longer she kept her eye open and focused on the clock, the less painful the experience became.

Alex had both eyes open now. Everything around her was blurry as she focused on the outline of the clock. She was tempted to look away and figure out what else she could see. Looking through her own eyes was exhilarating, and the pain was already more tolerable.

The dorm room door suddenly opened. Alex jumped at the sound and looked to see who had come in, which was a mistake. The moment she looked away from the clock, her eyes became overstimulated. A sharp pain pierced the back of her skull, and she fell from her chair.

"Who the hell is it?" Alex shouted.

No one answered. Finally, the intruder coughed loudly. "I just came in to check on you," Manny said. "It's about time we get you to training. First day and everything, you know?"

"Ugh. Manny, I'm going to need you to give me a hand with seeing again. I'm sorry."

"No worries, that's what I'm here for. We'll get you up and ready in no time."

Alex felt Jollies land on her shoulder. "Don't worry, Alex. We'll all help you," the pixie said. "Or at least me and Manny will. Now come on. We shouldn't be late."

CHAPTER THREE

Before Manny led Alex out of the room, he reestablished his psychic link with her eyes. The effect was uncomfortable, to say the least. Alex saw through her new eyes while simultaneously seeing through Manny's.

She stumbled out of the room, attempting to walk straight. She felt like all the descriptions of drunks she'd read about in her Victorian novels. The only difference was that she wasn't having anything close to a good time. Well, neither were the fictional drunks, at that level of intoxication.

After being hit with a wave of motion sickness worse than any she'd ever experienced, Alex leaned against the wall to catch her breath. "This isn't going to work, Manny," Alex said as she tried to steady herself.

Manny floated over to Alex and rested one of his tentacles on her shoulder. It was supposed to be a comforting gesture, but Manny's tentacles were somewhat slimy. "Don't worry, kid. We'll figure it out," he said.

"'Kid?' You sound like one of those old-time detectives from a film noir."

Manny smiled as some of his eyes widened. "That was a good time in human cinema," Manny laughed. "No one ever gets tired of Humphrey Bogart."

Alex stood straight and pulled her blindfold from her pocket. She tied it around her eyes so she only saw through Manny's eyes. "That's better." She sighed. "At least I'll be able to walk without falling over. So, where are we going?"

"First day is in the stables."

Alex did a double-take. "Wait, are you saying that the dragons are kept in stables?" she asked. "Some of the most ancient, dignified creatures of all time are kept in the same place as horses?"

He laughed at Alex's horror. "Trust me, you'll understand better when we get there," Manny said. "I don't want to ruin the surprise, but you're going to be glad you're picking up a few tricks."

He led them farther down the crystal halls, which shifted and contorted of their own accord. Even though Alex knew it was a bad idea, she was interested to know what the crystals would look like with her new eyes. Probably too beautiful to understand.

Manny, Alex, and Jollies rounded a corner, and the crystals pulled apart and created a large archway for them to walk through. Alex was still considering what Manny said about the stables.

It didn't make any sense for the dragons to be kept in stables. For one, the stables would have to be huge. Chine had been the smallest dragon, and he was twice the size of Alex's living room. The other dragons were nearly the size of a house.

Plainly put, Alex hadn't been expecting for her training to involve picking up dragon dung. The thought had never crossed her mind, and she realized right then and there that she couldn't think of anything she'd rather do less.

Not too high a price to pay to be in the sky, she reminded herself. *You've changed baby diapers before, and all infants ever do is look cute.*

Alex watched as the two crystal archways formed a set of double doors. To the right, the crystals produced a datapad. Manny floated over, ready to press his tentacles to the pad before he stopped and turned to Alex. "Actually, you should be all credentialed," he said.

She looked at the pad, which had changed so it had the imprint of a human hand. "What do you mean, credentialed?"

"You should be in the Nest's security system. As a dragonrider, you have access to most of the facility's operations and departments. The only place I know for sure you can't get into is the kitchen's storehouse after hours. Believe me, I've tried, but the kitchen is open twenty-four/seven anyway."

"So, I can come and go whenever I want?"

"Myrddin believes that our recruits should be treated with respect. We don't hold your hands, and we don't baby anyone. It should be refreshing."

Jollies flew over to Alex's left ear. "I've loved it," she whispered. "Supposedly, all we're supposed to do is train. The rest of the time is up to us."

"Do you really think they're stables? Like, for horses? I mean, I don't really want to pick up dragon turds. Don't get me wrong, I'll do it if I have to. It's just... Not that I was looking for something glamorous, but..."

"I was thinking the same thing. I can't imagine a dragon putting up with being confined to a stable, but who knows? Maybe they're really clean stables because we're the ones who'll be taking care of them."

Curiosity was getting the best of Alex, and she finally decided she didn't care if she was going to be cleaning up after her dragon. She only cared about flying again.

The dragons in *Middang3ard VR* had been nothing more than glorified steeds. Alex had been surprised when she heard Chine speak. The stables might be just as surprising.

She pressed her hand to the datapad; it was cold but instantly warmed at her touch. The doors to the dragon stables opened.

The first thing Alex noticed was how large the room was —easily the biggest room she'd been in so far. It was large in every sense of the word. The space gave you a bizarre feeling of having stepped into an infinite snow globe. Alex looked down as she walked. It felt as if the floor were sloping away from her.

As she got her bearings, she was able to take in more of her surroundings. "Stables" must have been a colloquial term for what the room actually was. It was split into multiple sections, most of which had a use Alex could not discern. Only the left part of the room was remotely identifiable. That section held a series of platforms, each big enough for the most massive dragon to rest upon comfortably.

Around the platforms were dozens of robotic arms with some kind of contraption attached to them.

Scientists zoomed by on floating scooters, taking notes or shouting at each other as they passed. It was that section Manny was leading Jollies and Alex toward.

Near the closest platform was a yeti standing nearly seven feet tall and covered in white fur. She wore nothing but a bandolier with a blaster and a rifle sheath attached. When she saw Alex and the other two approaching, she sneered and walked toward them.

Alex was surprised to see a yeti. She'd assumed the creatures that existed in Middang3ard were fantastical, like she'd read about in science fiction books. The thought reminded her of what Myrddin said about aliens and James Cameron, and suddenly yetis made much more sense.

The yeti raised her hand to Manny, showed her palm, and bowed slightly. Manny made a similar gesture with one of his tentacles. "Nice to see you three understand what being prompt means," Tribble growled.

Manny smiled and looked at his dragonriders. "These two do, at least," he said with a wink. "Neither of them could wait to get down here. Sally Tribble, meet Alex and Jollies."

Alex laughed. She really appreciated Manny trying to talk Jollies and her up. From Tribble's tone of voice, it seemed safe to assume Gill and Brath hadn't made it down to the stables yet.

Alex raised her hand to get Tribble's attention. The moment the yeti took notice of Alex's hand, the dragonrider regretted the action. Tribble stooped so she could look Alex in the eyes. "Are you in a classroom right now?" Tribble growled.

Alex swallowed hard as she prepared to answer. "I thought I was in something kind of like a classroom," she whispered. "I was just trying to get your attention without interrupting."

"That meek attitude is going to have to stop real soon. We can't afford dragonriders who waste valuable time being as polite as possible. If this is a classroom, it sure as hell isn't an etiquette lesson. Now, state your question."

"I was just going to ask about these being called stables, ma'am. Am I supposed to call you ma'am? I'm sorry. Never mind. These don't look like what I thought stables would look like."

"From what I've heard, how would you know what *anything* is supposed to look like?"

Alex flushed bright red as she tried to think of a retort. Tribble raised her hand, signaling to her to not even bother trying. "I don't have time for babysitting," the yeti said. "I'm assuming you can keep up since you're here, and I'll treat you thusly. Understood?"

Alex had heard of backhanded compliments, but this was something else entirely. She *was* happy Tribble didn't see her as some kind of helpless charity case. That was more than some of the other recruits thought of her. And it was exactly what Alex wanted: to be treated like everyone else.

Tribble turned and gestured toward the giant platforms with robotic arms. "This is one part of the stables," she explained. "Dragons are not horses or cattle. They are not restricted to a small area. If we did that, they would go insane and rampage through the Nest, killing everyone."

Tribble smiled, which was an odd look on her face. Her fierce black eyes glowed from behind a wall of white fur, and her sharp fangs glimmered. "They are dignified, majestic creatures," she continued. "Ours no less so because they were bred in captivity."

Alex's eyes widened as she tried to hold in her excitement. "Wait, you're saying that you guys bred these dragons?"

Tribble puffed out her chest, still smiling. "I'm saying that *I* bred these dragons, and I expect you all to take care of the dragons who bonded with you. Breeding was the only option for the program. A wild dragon hasn't chosen a rider in centuries, although I heard rumors of one doing that recently. But rumors are rumors."

Alex's heart was racing. She hadn't known dragons could be bred. And if getting chosen by a wild dragon was such a big deal, she wanted to meet the person who had. "So, if this place isn't for dragons...doing their business, what is it?"

"I'll wait until our new arrivals decide to *WALK FASTER AND JOIN US!*" Tribble shouted.

Alex jumped at her voice and turned to see Brath and Gill slinking toward the group. Brath didn't bother meeting her eyes, but Gill did. He nodded slightly in acknowledgment before standing next to her. Brath stood on Gill's other side.

Tribble paced up and down the line of new recruits. "Glad to see you felt like finally joining us," she snarled. "I'm guessing you missed the memo about promptness."

Brath sneered and said, "We didn't get here early to suck up to the instructor. Where is he, by the way?"

Tribble reached down and grabbed Brath by his shirt. "*She* is right here, Your Highness," she said before dropping Brath on his butt.

He scrambled to his feet and brushed off his clothes. "I'm sorry, ma'am. Didn't mean anything by it," he hurriedly apologized. "We got tied up talking to Myrddin. Won't happen again."

"I'll check on that story, but you better make sure it doesn't. Now, as I was telling Alex and Jollies, these are the dragons' stables. They are likely different from any stable you've seen so far. You will be cleaning up dragon waste, no doubt."

Alex felt the air depart her lungs as she settled back into reality. Maybe there was no way around cleaning up crap.

Tribble motioned for the cadets to follow her around the platforms. There, Alex could see that the robotic arms were actually attached to empty mechs. Each mech had a glass container on its backside.

Tribble climbed into one of the mechs and pushed her arms through the integration panel. She moved the mech's arm and picked up the glass container. "The cybernetic augments and armor that have been attached to the dragons create a kind of biological runoff," she explained.

Tribble shook the glass, and Alex could see it was filled with a clear liquid. "It is imperative that you take care of the health of your dragon," the yeti commanded. "They are sacrificing a lot for the sake of you riders."

"The augments provide stronger psychic connection for dragons and riders. They also enhance the dragon's speed, strength, and reflexes. And, since you are psychically connected, they improve yours as well. Now, these implants cause a lot of leakage, mostly blood and bodily fluid."

Tribble placed the glass on the ground and motioned for the cadets to step back. "The fluids are volatile and dangerous," she said as she cracked the glass with the mech's foot.

The liquid erupted into a green flame that shot into the air. "This will kill you if mishandled, but more importantly, it corrodes the dragon's armor, burns their skin, and harms them. So, first thing you're going to learn is how to take care of your mech. Suit up."

Alex went to the mech farthest from Brath and Gill. Manny followed a few feet behind her as she climbed inside. It felt snug when she slipped her arm into the integration panel.

A warm sensation flowed from the back of Alex's head, not unlike when she'd been connected to Chine. She didn't move the mech until she was ordered to by Tribble, though.

Tribble walked over to the cadets, holding two containers in her hand. A third container was attached to her back. "All right, each of you grab two containers and follow me," she ordered. "We're going to get rid of these before your dragons get back and we work with the real thing."

Alex did as she was told. Moving the mech wasn't difficult. It responded to her unconscious thoughts as if she were moving her own legs. She went to the two closest containers, picked them up, and lumbered after Tribble.

Tribble led them to a vat that was the size of a crater. Scientists were flying above it and taking notes, some of them flashing lights into the liquid. "This is the Stew," Tribble explained. "A collection of all dangerous fluids. Used mostly for incubation. We've also been researching dragon-blood-based weaponry. Should be ready by the time you're flying. Now come on. My babies should be getting back any moment."

Tribble dumped her containers into the Stew. Alex watched as the rest of the cadets did as well. Once they were all done, Alex moved over to the Stew and stared into it. The liquid looked like it was alive, sloshing around and almost reaching out for her. She opened her containers and dumped them.

She turned and jogged to rejoin the rest of the cadets. Brath was sneering at her as usual. "For someone who doesn't like me, you sure spend a lot of time looking at me," she chided.

Brath said nothing but scoffed loudly as he walked faster to catch up with Gill, who glanced over his shoulder at Alex but said nothing before turning back around.

Jollies pointed to the ceiling, which had peeled back so the sky could be seen. The dragons were coming. Alex could hardly contain herself. She wanted to jump up and down with excitement. Seeing the dragons flying toward her was magnificent. She held in her excitement, though.

Tribble walked past the cadets. The legs of her mech extended as she rose to the level of the pads. "All right," she said. "Get ready to greet your partners."

CHAPTER FOUR

Alex walked to Chine's landing platform as she watched the dragons dance. Dancing was the only word to explain it. They looked as if they were playing a game with each other in the clouds.

This was another reminder of how different the dragons of this realm were. Everything Alex had ever read about dragons stressed their serious nature and the dignified regality of their species. These dragons looked like teenagers joking around.

She scanned the area to see if the other cadets had gotten to their dragons' landing pads yet, which they had. Jollies was also staring at the dragons. Gill was exploring his mech, obviously unconcerned. Brath, on the other hand, was fussing with his mech quite a bit.

Chine shot a black jet of ether fire, and the rest of the dragons followed suit with their own elemental fire until the sky was filled with an explosion of color. After a moment, they raced toward their individual pads.

Alex had a sudden desire to run away. She'd seen dragons making this freefall dive in-game, and she'd always relished it as a chance to show off for the crowds around her. This time, it was apparent the display of power had nothing to do with her. It was all for the dragons' entertainment.

Chine led the charge toward Alex. At the last moment, he opened his wings and sent a gust of wind that almost knocked her out of her mech. Flapping his wings, he hovered above his landing pad for a second before touching down.

Mechanical pieces and armor covered the dragon's body. His head had been outfitted with something like a helmet, with a scanner stretched over one eye and tubes running from what looked like a dragon HUD into his mouth.

The rest of the armor was mostly weaponry. His shoulders were outfitted with plasma cannons, and his hands and feet were covered with energy claws. A crystal chest piece was also fitted with a cannon, and there was a spinal cover.

He looked like a frightening amalgamation of flesh and tech. Alex was glad the tech could be removed since the idea of a cyborg dragon made her queasy for some reason.

Chine's thoughts cut through Alex's. *Glad to see you made it to the first day of training, Dustling. It appears you are still adjusting to my sight. I must admit, I was very surprised to see you scream and faint. I assumed you were tougher.*

Alex started to say something but caught herself. Chine's voice hadn't been mocking. He was talking about her reaction in a very matter of fact way. Perhaps that was just the way dragons spoke. Maybe they didn't see the point of wasting time tap-dancing around feelings.

Alex coughed awkwardly as she tried to think of how to answer him. She looked around at the other cadets. All of them were silently staring at their dragons. *Guess everyone's doing introductions,* Alex thought before turning her attention back to Chine.

The dragon yawned lazily as he laid down and spread out his wings. *This will be the first time anyone other than my techni-*

cian has unloaded me. Please be careful of my scales. They are...
tender, to say the least.

Alex took a step toward Chine but stopped when she heard Tribble's whistle. She turned to the yeti, who was still in her mech. "All right," Tribble shouted, "let's start with the basics. First, we're removing the ocular devices. You're going to find a lot of leakage there. Do NOT touch it with your bare hands."

Alex nodded and grabbed her container as she stepped onto the landing pad. Her mech instantly compensated by extending its legs, and she shot up to Chine's eye level.

The dragon watched Alex without blinking. His serpentine eyes noted every one of her movements. *You are using the Beholder's eyes, are you not?* Chine asked.

Alex nodded, looking over her shoulder to where Manny was hanging out. She could see almost anything as long as the Beholder was in the room.

For now. She thought about how she could see through Chine's eyes too. And her own. *So many options. And to think, a few days ago, I had none.*

She reached out and took hold of the visor. When she tugged it gently, she could see where the tech was trying to fuse with Chine's scales. As she pulled, she positioned the container beneath the scanner, catching the sticky runoff from the dragon's scales. *Does it hurt?* she asked.

Chine snorted softly. *Does it matter if it hurts?*

I just mean, it looks very painful.

It is uncomfortable at times, but it's usually unnoticeable. It all depends on the technique of the attendant. Removal has the potential to hurt the most. You have the potential to hurt me the most. So, if you will, be as gentle as you can.

Using the strange magic of the Beholder's eyes, she checked around her to see how the other dragonriders were doing with their task.

Brath had wasted no time with Furi. He had already pulled off the dragon's headgear and was working on the shoulder cannons. Furi bristled and smoke floated from the dragon's nostrils as Brath worked on his armor, but otherwise, he didn't show any irritation.

Jollies, on the other hand, was having a much more interesting time with Amber. The dragon had shrunk somehow and was a fraction of the size Alex had initially seen. Amber was now roughly the volume of a puma, which was still huge for Jollies.

Amber had left the landing pad almost immediately after arriving. She was currently zipping around the stables at breakneck speed. Jollies was chasing her, laughing maniacally at this odd game of tag. It seemed like both of them were enjoying themselves.

Tribble was watching Jollies and Amber and shaking her head, obviously irritated.

Gill sat silently across from Timber. It looked like they were talking to each other. Gill hadn't removed any of Timber's armor but was seated closer to the dragon than Alex had seen anyone approach their steed so far.

Alex caught some of the fluid leaking from Chine's temple. *What's the best way to do this without hurting you?* she asked.

Slowly, Chine instructed. *As if you were peeling off a scab.*

Alex took Chine's advice to heart and slowly worked on removing the headgear. She could see why Chine had used a scab as an example. The skin was crusted underneath the headgear from the fluids burning through Chine's skin. It took a few minutes, but she was able to remove the tech piece.

She slipped her container next to Chine's temple and collected the oozing black fluid that seeped out of his cracked skin. *You have a knack for that, Dustling*, the dragon mused within Alex's head. *None of the technicians are as deft or considerate with their hands. I appreciate it.*

Chine stretched, letting a small amount of smoke float up from his nose. It reminded Alex of the way cats purr for some reason. *So,* Chine started, *you're having a hard time using the sight Myrddin gave you? Seeing with your own eyes?*

Alex moved on to Chine's shoulder cannons. She stretched out one of the robotic tools and wedged it between the flesh and tech, slowly prying the two apart. *I'm trying to see. Trying as hard as I can. It's just, it feels like it's too much. Manny's eyes are more manageable.*

But Manny won't be with us always. Hopefully not, at least. I've heard Beholders make terrible riders. They have no hands. He let out a puff of smoke as a strange gurgling came from him.

A dragon's laugh? Alex wondered.

Chine sat up while Alex was working, forcing her to extend her mech's legs to stay close to his shoulders. *Perhaps now would be a good time to practice,* Chine suggested. *You are handling extremely dangerous fluids. Not burning yourself would make a good incentive.*

Alex stared at Chine in disbelief. "Wait, are you kidding me?" Alex yelped. "Why would you—"

Alex didn't get a chance to finish her sentence. The world around her was suddenly disorienting. She was looking straight ahead, but where she was looking had nothing to do with her eyes. Then the view slowly turned to the left, and Alex was staring at herself.

She started to scream but caught it in her throat as she began to lose her balance and fall. She grabbed the dragon's shoulder with the mech's hand and steadied herself.

Chine looked away, laughing again. *I apologize. I didn't think about how disorienting it would be to see yourself through my eyes.*

The wave of disorientation left Alex. She was glad

Chine had turned away so quickly. If he hadn't, Alex might have fallen and dropped all of Chine's liquids. "Jesus, you need to warn me before you do something like that," she shouted.

He blew out smoke as he stretched out. *Okay, what about Furi's eyes?* Chine asked.

What do you mean?

This time Alex braced herself against Chine's shoulder and shut her eyes tight. That didn't stop her from seeing, though. She was looking through Furi's eyes at Brath, who was petting the top of the dragon's nose.

Or better yet, Chine continued, *what about Timber?*

Alex's vision switched again, and she held onto Chine's shoulder as tightly as she could. She—or her eyes, at least—were zooming around faster than she could follow. It had to be Amber, who was flying as fast as she could, looping through the legs of the scientists and around crystal columns.

Motion sickness hit Alex hard, and she had to focus on not throwing up. "Chine, stop it. This is not funny," she muttered.

Chine chuckled, and Alex forced herself to concentrate on getting back onto solid ground. She directed her mech off the landing pad, and once it was stationary, she jumped out and landed on the stable floor.

The last thing Alex saw before her eyesight returned to normal was Tribble looking at her, shaking her head. If Alex had seen that through her own eyes, she wouldn't have thought twice, but through Chine's eyes, Alex could see the disappointment on the yeti's face.

Not knowing what to do, Alex ripped off her blindfold. She had the feeling that if she was looking through her own eyes and not Manny's, the dragon wouldn't be able to mess with her perspective as much. She didn't quite understand why, but as soon as the blindfold came off, she was no longer connected to Manny.

It was her eyes and nothing else.

The initial shock of light threw Alex off-guard, but she was relieved to find that she could see what was directly in front of her. She blinked a few times before the pain started to set in, and an idea hit her: she could adjust the HUD to dim the light, so to speak. When she did, it was as if she were looking through thin fabric, which was much more manageable.

Once she had oriented herself, she said to Chine, *How about you stop with the pranks and we just get to work?*

Chine was still gurgling softly.

Alex climbed back into her mech and sprang up to Chine's shoulders. *Unless you want this to be more 'uncomfortable' than when the technicians are working on you,* she threatened.

Chine's laughter died instantly. *Well, Dustling, I'm glad to see you're not as timid as you seem.*

Was that what this was about? You wanted to see if I'm timid?

Chine shot a short jet of ether fire from one of his nostrils. Alex jumped at both the sound of the fire and the heat. The dragon looked at her and smiled. *Timidity is not an attribute that would help on the battlefield,* he mused.

I'm not timid. Now let's hurry up and get this over with.

Alex started peeling off Chine's armor again. She wished she had something more biting to say to him. Even worse, though, she was annoyed that she not only had to prove herself to the other cadets, but apparently to her dragon as well. Was anyone going to cut her any slack?

Chine stretched out his arm, making it easier for Alex to get to the shoulder cannons. *I mean no disrespect,* he explained. *I have had many a failed rider. It would be best not to lose another.*

"Maybe if you tried talking to them instead of putting them through a gauntlet of stupid tests, you might be able to hold on to one," Alex spat.

Chine laughed heartily as he stretched out a little more. *Perhaps. Perhaps.*

Alex finally managed to pull off the shoulder cannon and catch the fluid in one of the containers before Tribble called the cadets back.

Tribble instructed them to dump the contents in the Stew. After the cadets were done, she explained to them that they were going to have to do this with much less tech on the field. She showed them smaller fluid-draining devices and the apparatus they could use to absorb and store the fluid.

Brath held up one of the syringes. "How exactly are we supposed to use these?"

Tribble walked up to Brath and flicked his head. "You climb on your dragon, wedge this between the armor, and pull back the plunger," she growled. "That make enough sense?"

"You mean, I have to climb—"

"If that doesn't work for your sensibilities, perhaps you have a servant who could help?"

Brath blushed brightly and turned away from Tribble, looking at his syringe.

Alex leaned over to Jollies and whispered, "Why does Tribble keep saying things like that?"

Jollies grinned and flew over to Alex's ear. "Brath doesn't want anyone to know, but he's gnomish royalty. You can't tell anyone."

Alex nodded, happy she had gotten some dirt on the gnome, but she didn't have much time to enjoy the tiny preemptive victory since Tribble was already rushing them back to their dragons.

Alex walked up to Chine, explained the situation, and

asked if she could climb on top of him. He said it was no problem. It took Alex some time to find the best way to make her way onto the dragon, but after a few attempts, she was scrambling around, trying to pry Chine's tech up enough to slip in the syringe.

Before Alex could freak out about scampering around on a dragon, a thought crossed her mind. *Hey, how did you make me see through everyone's eyes?*

Chine pulled up his hind leg to scratch the back of his neck. *Ether dragons, and I in particular, are very strong psychics,* he explained. *We attach bonds to everyone around us and can access them easily, although none of those bonds will be as strong as ours. Who knows? That psychic ability might rub off on you as well; it's not unheard of. Still, it's unusual for the bond to work so well. Usually, there is some resistance. I don't know if you so readily receive my signals because you're human or because you're blind.*

Hmm, maybe both? Alex offered and she continued to ask Chine questions about the nature of his ability. He seemed much more inclined to talk than to pull pranks at the moment. The conversation carried on easily as Alex became more comfortable moving across the dragon.

Draining all his fluid took nearly the entire day. There were slip-ups, obviously. Jollies had managed to lose some of Amber's armor. Brath had said something to Furi to make the dragon shoot off a couple of fireballs that scorched the gnome's eyebrows.

The only cadet who hadn't had any noticeable issues with their dragon was Gill. The two worked together seamlessly, and he was the first cadet to be done with the draining.

The rest of the cadets finished at roughly the same time.

Alex leaped off Chine and sighed with exhaustion. She'd never been very physical, and scrambling around Chine was on a par with rock climbing. After Alex dumped her syringe, she came back to the dragon and sat down in front of him. *Thanks for talking to me*, she said. *And for cutting out all that nonsense.*

Chine leaned his head forward until he was staring into Alex's eyes. *You are an interesting cadet*, he admitted. *I have never met a human. There are still some...cultural differences we'll have to explore, but you seem like you'll be a good rider. I believe our binding was wise.*

Alex, who was unprepared to have gotten such a sincere response, laughed nervously before extending her hand to Chine. "Me too," she blurted. "I'm really looking forward to it."

He laughed when he saw Alex's hand and took it between his fingers. They shook, and he laid down. *You should get some rest*, he suggested. *We'll see each other soon.*

Alex nodded before walking off. Manny followed behind her. "Oh, snap, Manny. I forgot you were here."

Manny's tentacled eyes swung around widely. "Don't worry about it. I was partially here. We Beholders are able to see many different realms of reality. I can keep myself entertained. Now let's get some grub!"

Alex yawned and stretched. "To be honest, I'm way too tired for that." She put on the blindfold and connected through Manny's eyes. It was a relief. "Do you think you could just escort me to my room, and I'll catch you tomorrow?"

Manny nodded. "Up to you." They continued down the hall to Alex's room, where she said goodbye and shut the door behind her.

There was much Alex wanted to think through. Spending an afternoon with Chine had been more interesting than she expected. She hadn't thought the dragon would act like a teenager after all his dignified words.

But there wasn't time to think about that; she was hardly

able to make it to her bed. She changed into her pajamas and collapsed onto her sheets.

She woke to Jollies zipping around the room and singing surprisingly loud for such a small creature. Alex put her pillow over her head. She wanted a couple more minutes of sleep. It was amazing how big a difference five minutes made.

As Alex tried to drift back to sleep, she felt a tug on her pillow. It must have been a polite warning because the next second, Alex's pillow was ripped off her head. "Okay, okay," Alex shouted. "I'm up. Why are you in such a chipper mood?"

Jollies stopped flying for a second, stunned. She pointed at Alex's desk. There was a plate of eggs, bacon, and potatoes waiting for her. "Just thought you might want to have something to eat before class."

Alex wanted to kick herself. Jollies was trying to be a great roommate, and Alex had already filled the position of the grouchy one. "I'm sorry, Jollies," Alex started. "I'm just not a morning person. I didn't mean to bite your head off."

Jollies shook off the pained look on her face and replaced it with a beaming smile. "Oh, don't worry about it," she said. "I'm not a night person. Don't even try to talk to me after midnight."

"Midnight? That's hardly early. What time do you wake up?"

"Around sunrise, like most pixies. The sun pulls us out of bed."

Alex rolled off her bed and grabbed her sweater. Her head was beginning to hurt. That was when she realized she'd opened her eyes and looked around the room without any problem. It was only now that they were starting to irritate her.

The blindfold was on the floor. Alex grabbed it, shook it off, and then wrapped it around her head. She peered through the fabric, silently congratulating herself. It looked like she was starting to get used to the intensity of her new eyesight.

She stumbled over to her plate of food and dug in. She didn't bother talking until she was finished.

Jollies sat on the side of Alex's desk, watching her eat. When Alex was finished, Jollies swooped over and grabbed a small piece of leftover bacon. "You really get hungry, don't you?" the pixie asked.

"Not usually. Just since I got here. Guess it's stress-eating. So, how was working with Amber for the first time?"

Jollies smile disappeared for a moment. "She is *difficult*," Jollies admitted. "She didn't want to do anything Tribble was trying to get us to do. I spent most of the day chasing her around, and when we finally got to remove the armor, all she did was complain. This wasn't what I was expecting."

"Me either," Alex admitted. "I remember reading about how noble dragons were."

"I ran into Tribble and got to talk to her a little bit after class. Apparently, these are very young dragons, and since they weren't raised by other dragons, their temperaments are different. They're pretty much like dragon children, maybe even younger than us."

"Interesting. That would explain a lot. So, what are we up to today?"

"We have class. Introduction to Dragon Hybrid Technologies and Their Practical Applications."

Alex stretched before scraping the last of her food off her plate. "That's a mouthful." She sighed.

Jollies zipped around the room to her dresser, which

hung from the wall, stepped behind a curtain, and changed. "I think Dragon Tech 101 will do," she suggested.

Alex grabbed her sweater off the floor and changed from her pajamas to her pants. She hit her dragon anchor, and her rider armor, composed of nanobots, rippled over her. "Hey, did you happen to talk to Gill today?" she asked.

Jollies poked her head out from behind her curtain. "Why are you asking?" she said, smiling mischievously.

"Just curious to know how another cadet felt about everything. I'm not interested in knowing what Brath thinks until he stops being such a jerk."

"Makes sense. I'm not really keen on talking to Brath either. He's nice enough to me, but he's such a tool to you. But no, I haven't had a chance to talk to Gill. He doesn't seem like he does much talking."

Alex checked the time on her dragon anchor. It was getting close to ten. She couldn't believe she'd slept so late. "What time are we supposed to be in class?"

Jollies zipped out from behind her changing curtain and hit her dragon anchor. Her armor slid over her body as she spun in the air. "Around ten-thirty. Ready to go?"

They found the classroom for Dragon Tech 101 easily enough. Alex was getting used to navigating the confusing hallways of the Wasp's Nest. It helped that Manny was along every step of the way.

The Beholder had met the two girls outside their dorm room as they left. He didn't seem particularly talkative, and Alex remembered what he'd said the day before. There was a good chance his attention was on another realm of reality.

Glad he's keeping himself busy, Alex thought. *I was starting to feel bad for the poor guy, having to follow me around everywhere.*

Alex considered telling him she could see through Chine's eyes and her own, if she adjusted her HUD to dim things, but she didn't. She wasn't quite ready to let Manny go yet. As selfish as it might be, she couldn't discount that she was on a whole new world learning insane things. She deserved another few days of support.

Didn't she?

Once the dragonriders got to their class, they went inside and took seats in the second row. This class was much larger than their class in the stables. There were at least twenty empty seats. They were still a couple of minutes early.

Around 10:25, the other cadets started to fill the room.

Brath and Gill were among the last to enter. Brath glared at Alex as he walked by. Gill passed Alex without acknowledging her and her heart sank, but she tried to ignore it.

Samantha Choice, their professor according to Manny, entered the room at 10:30 on the dot. She was a tall human with curly bright red hair. She wore the armor of a MECH rider, and her glasses matched the deep red suit. Unlike anyone else in the class, her armor had a collection of badges over her heart.

Choice smiled at the class before taking a seat at her desk in the front of the classroom. She hit her temple HUD and began calling roll. Each student answered in turn, and when Choice got to Alex's name, she looked up and smiled.

Once roll was done, Choice wasted no time getting to the meat of the class. She projected a large holograph of a handful of dragons and lectured on the history of the "bionic augments" being used on them. She warned the students against using a term like "tech" or "mech."

Choice pointed at a shoulder cannon and told them, "'Bionic' is the proper term for what we've created for these dragons. It is a combination of living tissue, tech, and magic

—the best of each, and we are still refining it. Here are other examples of the bionics we use."

The holograph changed, showing an underwater breathing apparatus. "Only a few dragon breeds are capable of surviving underwater," Choice explained. "The lack of air and substantially increased pressures can burst the dragons' lungs, which are quite delicate."

Choice swiped right on the holograph to a similar breathing device. "From underwater bionics, we've also created some that allow our dragons and riders to breathe in space for limited amounts of time while equalizing rider and dragon body pressures."

The professor swiped to another holograph as Alex leaned back in her chair. *Wow, she's just going to plow through this, isn't she?* she thought.

Her assumption was correct. Choice continued to scroll through bionic piece after bionic piece. Many of them put what Alex had seen in *Middang3ard* the game to shame. The game only had what Choice would have called basic armor and weapons.

The upgrades Choice showed them ranged from bionic pieces attached to the spine to increase speed and flight stability or internal implants to allow dragons to change their elemental attacks.

Alex's favorite bionic piece was a scale refractor invented based on experiments done with octopi. The piece allowed a dragon to control each individual scale for unparalleled camouflage capabilities.

Choice turned off her holoprojector as she sat down and crossed her legs. "These bionic upgrades are available to our top-tier riders," she explained. "The higher you go in our ranks, the more access you have. The best bionics go to the best riders. Do you understand?"

The class filled with murmurs of assent and agreement.

"All right," Choice shouted. "Break for lunch and head to your next class."

The cadets all got out of their seats and made their way to the door. As Alex went to depart, she felt a hand on her shoulder. She turned to see that it was Choice. "Hold back for a second," the teacher requested.

Alex stood off to the side and watched the rest of her classmates leave. She tried to avoid Gill's and Brath's eyes.

Once the cadets had cleared out, Choice motioned for Alex to come to her desk. "I just wanted to give you some tips," she explained. "Don't get dragged down by being human here, all right?"

Alex didn't understand what Choice meant. She'd been more concerned about being the blind girl than being human. "What do you mean?" she asked.

"First-year cadets always have a problem mixing. You're going to get hazed. Just remember, by the end of the first year, there aren't elves, gnomes, or dwarves. There are dragonriders, and that's it. Whoever fails to grasp that won't make it. Do you understand? You ever need anything, just let me know. Now get the hell out of here and eat some food."

Alex didn't waste any time leaving Choice's classroom. She was a little too intense for her. Manny was waiting outside the door and followed Alex as she tried to navigate to the mess hall. It took time, but she found it soon enough.

The cadets had already split into their cliques. Alex didn't want to wait around and see where she was going to sit, so she grabbed her food and found a place away from the crowd. After a couple of minutes, Jollies flew over and sat with her.

She put her plate on the table as a few other pixies came over to join them. "I was wondering what was taking you so long," Jollies said. "Hey, guys. This is Alex."

The small group introduced themselves, but before they

could say more, Alex felt eyes staring at her. She turned to find Brath behind her. "Can I help you with something?" she asked.

Alex couldn't stand to look at Brath and that ridiculous beard of his.

Even though Alex knew Brath was her age, the beard gave him the appearance of a very grouchy old man. "What's with your HUD?" Brath asked. "It's all misty, like you're wearing a blindfold or something."

Alex looked at the other cadets. People were starting to take notice. This would become a scene shortly. She knew enough about high school to recognize that this was a defining moment for how the rest of the cadets would see her. "I'm kind of blind," Alex said, "if you haven't noticed."

"Was that what Choice wanted to talk to you about? Give you special attention because you're the little blind girl?"

Alex scoffed and turned back to her food. "You already used that one, Brath. If you don't have anything original to waste my time with, you can leave."

Brath stood there, his jaw slack with surprise. "Don't you talk to me like that, human!" he shouted.

"Oh, a jab against me being human? Didn't see that one coming. You want to make fun of me for being a girl next, or have you run out of crappy tropes?"

Brath stood there in silence for a while, then folded his arms and walked off as the rest of the cadets started to snigger. Soon they lost interest, and a few even patted Alex on the back as they passed her.

After the cadets cleared out, Alex could see Gill watching from a distance. Their eyes met, and Alex felt her face flush as he unceremoniously walked off, leaving her alone with the butterflies in her stomach.

Alex had to attend one more class before the day was over. Jollies, Manny, and Alex headed to the Introduction to Dragons class.

Most of the cadets from the previous class and lunch were in the classroom already. Brath was nowhere to be seen. Gill was sitting at the back of the room, staring into the distance. Alex had a very difficult time taking her eyes off him.

Fier Timles walked into the room. Alex was confused as to the teacher's species. Fier's skin was scaly like a dragon's, as were most of the facial features.

Two long horns stretched from Timles' forehead to lower back.

A long, thin robe covered the body and wrapped around the neck. Fier was extremely slender and looked more like a snake than a dragon. Alex couldn't discern the teacher's gender, but she decided Fier must be female. Any creature with so many amazing curves must be female. Maybe there weren't any differences for her race.

Fier took a seat at her desk and put up her feet. "All right, this is one of your prerequisites," she droned. "Not my favorite class to teach because it's boring as all hell, but we'll go ahead and get through the worst of it."

A holographic image of a dragon appeared in front of the classroom. "Take notes if you want," she said. "There might be a test or something. Here's your first type of dragon: classic red. They're what everyone thinks of when they hear 'dragon.'"

Fier went through each slide, pointing out the differences between species of dragon. It wasn't anything particularly new to Alex. There was a lot of talk about dragon biology, but Alex didn't pay close attention. The teacher didn't look excited about delivering the lecture, so it couldn't be too important.

The lecture about the various species was straightforward. Lightning dragons were born of thunder and lightning and were partially composed of electricity. Fire dragons were cousins of red dragons, being born in fire and commanding the power of flames to lesser or greater degrees.

Earth dragons struck Alex as interesting. They seemed to have the least elemental power, and Fier rushed through their description quickly. Alex cast a look over her shoulder to see if Gill was paying attention.

Gill was balancing his pencil on his fingertip. He looked up and caught Alex staring, and he placed his pen back on the table and turned to gaze straight ahead at Fier.

"Now, ether dragons have an interesting history," Fier continued.

Alex's ears perked up, and she turned her attention back to Fier's holographic slideshow. "Even less is known about ether dragons than earth dragons. We know that they're the youngest species, and their elemental properties fluctuate greatly from dragon to dragon."

Fier switched images again, showing an ether dragon amid a massive explosion. "We've read tales of ether dragons able to create some kind of gravitational vortex, which could allude to the real source of the dragons' power. The last story of that happening was a couple thousand years ago, though. It doesn't seem like any living ether dragon knows about this ability."

The class continued for almost three hours, and the teacher took no breaks. She described species after species. There were many more species of dragons, drakes, and wyrms than Alex would have ever guessed.

At the end of the class, Fier packed her bag, turned to the cadets, and said, "All right, there you go. Learning everything you can about every kind of dragon isn't going to help any of you. Research your individual dragon and go from there.

Read your textbook. Next class is…I don't know, I'll email you or something."

Fier rushed out of the class faster than any of the students.

Jollies flew over to Alex, giggling. "Guess dragonriders aren't much for theory, huh?" she asked.

The two walked out of the room and went over to where Manny was waiting. "Guess not," Alex agreed. "Thank God, because that was the most boring class I've ever sat through in my entire life."

Around dinnertime, the cadets started to pour out of their rooms. Alex went to the mess hall with Jollies, but after she grabbed her meal, she told the pixies she had planned to video chat with her parents around that time and left the mess hall as fast as possible. She hadn't made any plans to talk with her parents; avoiding a repeat of her last meal was her real plan. A meal alone sounded refreshing.

Once Alex was back in her room, she changed into her pajamas, crawled into bed, and pulled up her HUD as she ate. She searched through the different textbooks uploaded onto her HUD until she found Fier's textbook, *A History of Dragon Species*.

Alex opened the book and lost herself as she slowly worked her way through her meal. By the time she finished, it was only 8pm. *Whatever*, Alex thought. *I deserve an early night.*

CHAPTER FIVE

The next morning, Jollies and Manny led Alex down various hallways to the training yard, where the Nest opened to a field that stretched as far as she could see. Well, see through Manny's eyes, at least.

There were more cadets than Alex had seen before. It seemed as if the whole field was filled with people of various ages. The oldest one Alex saw was a dwarf who might be in his sixties.

Fier and Tribble were separating cadets by groups, which Alex noted ran from their year in the academy up to fourth. Jollies explained that some cadets were able to skip grades. They graduated to the next year based on performance, not age.

Once the two instructors had the cadets sectioned off, Tribble took all the cadets who were second years and up and headed toward a forest that loomed ominously in the distance. The rest of the cadets would be training with Fier, and she had them line up.

Fier paced up and down the two rows of students. There were at least twenty first-year cadets, and the teacher did not look impressed with any of them. "All right, all of you have been bound to a dragon," she started. "And all of you have experience on top of a dragon in some regard."

Fier stopped to look at Alex for a moment. "Even if some of you have only practiced in VR, you'll catch on eventually. Do you have any questions?"

A young, black-haired elvish male raised his hand. "Er, ma'am? What exactly are we going to be doing?"

"The first thing you're going to do is pay attention! You got that?"

He slunk back and hung his head. Fier smiled. "All right, so the first thing you're going to do is call your dragon down to you. After that, you're going to have thirty minutes of free airtime. That's exactly what it sounds like, but I want you back here in thirty minutes. Then it's the obstacle course. You got it?"

"Yes, ma'am!" the cadets shouted.

Fier raised her dragon-anchor arm. "Raise your arm, and that'll activate your dragon anchor," she commanded. "Then you concentrate and call to your dragon. How well they hear you is determined by your binding, which is determined by the relationship between the two of you. Understood?"

"Yes, ma'am!"

Fier's dragon anchor lit up and flashed a vibrant red light. In the distant sky, a bright twinkling was visible. Within seconds, a red dragon came screeching from the sky and landed directly in front of the teacher. The force of the dragon's impact shook the earth, causing some of the cadets to fall.

Fier leaped into the air and landed atop her dragon. She held her hand over the dragon's neck, and her anchor glowed. "No fighting whatsoever!" she shouted. "I don't want you to even look at each other in the air. Respect each other's space and get used to riding."

Fier's dragon spread its wings and took to the air without giving any of the cadets a second look.

The cadets glanced at each other, unsure of who was going to be the first to call their dragon. Finally, a dwarf walked away and raised his dragon anchor to the sky. He stood there for some time before he realized that his dragon wasn't coming. He slunk back to the crowd.

Brath laughed obnoxiously before he walked away from the rest of the cadets. He raised his dragon anchor, which glowed bright red. There was a vicious roar from above as the clouds parted.

Furi, the red fire dragon, came plummeting down with his wings curled around his body. He only spread them at the last minute, creating a gust of wind that knocked over a few cadets as he unleashed a plume of fire from his mouth. Furi reached down and opened his hand for Brath to climb into, and the two took off.

Alex leaned over to speak to Manny, who was floating next to her. "Hey, do you think we could get away from the rest of them? I don't really want to do this with everyone watching, and I have to take you up there with me and everything." She thought about leaving him behind and using Chine's eyes or her own, but decided against it. She wasn't quite ready.

You'll have to do it sooner or later, she admonished herself.

Later.

Manny nodded, his eyes drooping. "Yeah, I know I gotta go with you," he grumbled as they walked off.

"Hey, I'm sorry. I know this must be getting old and—"

"Oh, it's not you, kid. I don't mind helping you. It's just that I'm not one for flying, if you haven't noticed. No legs and arms, you know. Hard to keep from getting sick. But don't worry. I'm here to help you."

Once Alex was happy with the amount of distance she'd

put between her and the other cadets, she raised her dragon anchor. *All right, Chine*, she thought, directing her intent to the dragon. *I hope you can hear me.*

Alex's dragon anchor glowed a deep, violent black. There was a loud shriek from the sky, and a bright black light flashed. Alex watched as Chine came flying toward her. He was nothing more than a black streak and was moving faster than she'd ever imagined a dragon could.

Chine hit the ground and skidded across it. His claws dragged and tore up the grass as he tossed his head back and shrieked loudly, calling the attention of every cadet who hadn't managed to summon their dragon yet. *Gods*, finally. Chine sighed. *I thought you would stay down here all day!*

Alex couldn't help but smile. This was the first time Chine seemed happy to see her. *It's good to see you too*, she replied.

Chine leaned to the side, spreading his right wing out so Manny could float up it. He pulled his wing back quickly. *You, on the other hand, are going to have to get up here yourself.*

How am I going to do that? Alex asked.

Just jump!

Alex took a deep breath. Chine was easily six feet taller than her, but maybe the dragon knew something she didn't. It was about time to start trusting him. She crouched and then exploded upward, and landed on Chine's back. She instinctively reached down to catch herself, her dragon anchor locking her feet and hands to the dragon.

Chine laughed heartily. *That's what I like to see. Now let's get into the air.*

Uh, how do I do that?

You know exactly how to do that.

Alex nodded, trying to invoke all the muscle memory from when she was in VR. In this place, she was strong enough to pull off such a feat.

She pulled her dragon anchor back, which caused Chine to rear up on his hind legs. Alex spread her feet apart from each other and pushed forward. Chine spread his wings and flapped them to take off.

He soared into the air as Alex pushed the dragon to go faster. The wind whipped Alex's face, making its way through her HUD and blindfold and bringing tears to her eyes.

Guess these eyes are working just the way they should, she mused as she focused on seeing through Manny's eyes only. The Beholder's eyes didn't tear up like hers. *Another benefit of being a magical creature, huh?* she thought.

Alex felt like she was going to slip right off Chine. Her heart was racing as she struggled against the wind.

It was so different from being in VR. The speed, the wind, and the chill were all unexpected. She wasn't sure if she enjoyed it, but this was what she was here for.

She pulled her dragon anchor to the right, and Chine followed her lead by barreling with closed wings before free-falling.

If Alex could deal with a free fall, she'd be able to deal with anything. Behind her, Manny was attached to her like a baby in a backpack, screaming over the wind.

Chine laughed again, the hearty noise ringing in Alex's head. *Don't you think this is a little advanced for you, Dustling?* he asked.

Alex concentrated on listening to the wind and the way it rang in her ears. She knew how to do this. She *knew* she knew how to do this. *Aren't we supposed to trust each other?*

Well said, Alex. Well said.

The ground was fast approaching. Alex could see the specks she knew to be her classmates. She didn't want to get too close. She wasn't trying to scare them.

Or worse, embarrass herself.

Alex pulled back on the dragon anchor and Chine spread his wings and came to a complete stop, jerking Alex forward and almost knocking her off-balance.

Her dragon floated in midair, a safe distance from her fellow cadets. *Well done, Dustling. Well done*, the dragon boomed in her mind.

She raised the dragon anchor and Chine took off, soaring into the sky but slower than before. She was starting to get a handle on how the slightest movement from her dragon anchor hand guided Chine's speed and direction.

She could slow down, speed up, and turn with the most minuscule of movements.

The two lazily floated through the sky and Alex watched the sun filter through the white clouds. For the first time since Alex had arrived at the Wasp's Nest, she felt like she belonged.

She lost track of how long she was up there. Chine was singing softly under his breath, but Alex didn't hear his tune in her mind. She felt it coming from him, his whole body vibrating with his low hum.

Her HUD dinged loudly, and she opened a message from Fier. It was time to come down for the second part of the day: the obstacle course.

She guided Chine back down to the ground and he landed beside Timber, Gill's earth dragon. Gill briefly acknowledged Alex and then turned his attention back to Fier, who had just landed.

Fier pointed at an obstacle course that had been magically set up in the sky. It was difficult to tell what each section was because it was so far away, and Manny's eyes were apparently not made for long distances.

Jollies found her way to Alex and stared at the course as well. Fier's voice rang out over the cadets talking or murmuring. "All right, these are timed runs. Think of this as a race. You'll go through it alone, but we're scoring you against each other. First up, Gill."

Alex watched as Gill's dragon Timber took off into the sky. It was difficult to see what he was doing with Manny's eyes. She thought about asking Chine to look through his, but it was all becoming too much. Alex had gone from having no eyes to having three sets—her own, Manny's, and Chine's—and she still didn't feel comfortable with any of them.

Chine's voice broke through Alex's anxiety. *Ah, one of these. I've seen the other dragons do them before. They seem...somewhat pointless.*

Alex giggled in her head. *Why do you think that?*

I doubt any obstacles we find on the battlefield will be so simply laid out.

One by one, the other cadets were called to the air and finished the course. After nearly twenty minutes, Alex was the last one. Fier called her name, and Alex raised her dragon anchor.

Chine shot toward the first large circle as fast as he could. Once he passed through the hoop, a dozen more appeared to their right. Some of them were on fire, others moving. "Looks easy enough," she said, racing toward them.

As Alex flew, her vision blurred. *Manny must be getting motion-sick again,* she thought.

Alex passed through the next hoop and went for the third one. As she got closer, the circle turned and a blaster popped out from its side. She swerved to the right to avoid the blast. "What the hell was that?" she shouted.

Chine rolled to the other side, doubled back, and dove through the hoop, which caused four more to appear below them, each covered in blasters. *Don't all obstacle courses have a threat of death?* he asked.

Alex went for the closest hoop, reached instinctively

toward Chine's left wing, and fired his shoulder cannon. Likewise, Chine shot a jet of ether fire, scorching the blasters. Alex pushed forward to gain speed, but Manny's vision blurred again.

The world descended into darkness for a second as Manny leaned over the dragon's side and threw up.

He righted himself, and Alex's vision snapped back into place. She saw she'd overshot the hoops, so she pulled hard to the right, and Chine swerved with her while firing another plume of ether fire to knock out a plasma blast coming their way. *Thank God Chine knows what he's doing,* she thought.

Alex managed to move through each of the hoops and slowed drastically so Manny wouldn't get sick enough to black out again. After Alex passed through the last hoop, she looked around to locate more. Once she was satisfied they were done, they headed back to the rest of the cadets.

A holographic bulletin board was floating in front of Fier. The times of the other cadets were posted. Alex pushed her way to the front to see where she was listed.

Alex Bound. Her name was all the way at the bottom—the slowest time of any of the cadets. *There's no way I'm going to be able to live this down,* Alex thought as she slunk away from the other cadets, avoiding their eyes. *See you later, Chine,* Alex thought as she waved at the dragon.

Chine bowed politely, his eyes dancing. *You shouldn't think anything of it, Dustling,* Chine told her. *None of the other cadets are working under your conditions.*

Thanks.

Chine took off when Fier dismissed the cadets for the day. Alex intentionally tried to avoid Jollies as she made her way back to her room, where she laid on her bed and pulled her pillow over her head. At least the day was over.

CHAPTER SIX

A lex woke with a headache. It wasn't anything new, but that wasn't what was keeping Alex from getting out of bed. She kept replaying the race from the day before. She could see Brath's sneering face peering at her from underneath his beard.

Losing to Brath would have been bad enough, and that in itself was humiliating. Coming in last was too much to deal with, though. Alex had never lost anything to that extent before. She wanted to be a good dragonrider so badly.

She rolled over in bed and pulled her covers over her eyes. *I thought that Myrddin said VR was supposed to be like pre-training,* Alex thought. *Doesn't feel like I'm remotely ready for any of this.*

She tried to remember lessons she'd learned from *Middang3ard VR*, anything that would transfer over to help her with the issues she was currently experiencing. She couldn't think of anything.

Middang3ard VR hadn't been a particularly encouraging place in-game. The game world was somewhat pessimistic.

Most of the hope and joy players found was from relation-ships built with other players, something Alex significantly lacked in real life.

Jollies seemed like the only person who was still inter-ested in helping Alex or making her feel at home. Manny had just about checked out, relegating himself to a pair of floating eyes, probably watching inter-realm television in his head or something like that.

Alex thought maybe she should put forth more of an effort to talk to Manny and see if he had any insight on the situation. He was an eldritch creature and might have some kind of wisdom to drop on her.

That was when Alex remembered she hadn't talked to her parents about any of this. She'd completely forgotten they were only a phone call away. All she had to do was send them a message.

Alex pulled down her HUD and scrolled through its options until she found the messaging option. She picked the video message option. A mirrored screen of herself showed on her HUD. Alex tried to fix her hair and did her best to smile. "Hey, Mom. Hey, Dad," Alex started.

She deleted the video and started again, forcing a more organic smile. "Hey, guys, just wanted to say hi. Haven't talked to you in a bit, and I miss you."

Alex's brave front fell apart quickly. She realized she'd never really had friends before. Her parents were pretty much all she'd had until she'd started playing *Middang3ard*, and even then, it was just Jim. It wasn't all the teasing that was getting to Alex. It was loneliness.

Tears welled up in Alex's eyes, and she didn't bother trying to fight them. She just wiped them off as she talked. "Yeah, it's pretty lonely here," Alex cried. "My roommate is pretty cool, but she has all her friends and stuff and, I don't know; some people are real jerks just because I'm blind and human. I don't know which one is worse for them. So, I guess I don't know. What would you guys do? I'm kinda at a loss here. All right. Looking forward to hearing from you guys. I love you a lot."

Alex disconnected the HUD and pulled her sheets back over her head. Being lonely was harder when you were around other people. She hadn't realized she'd missed out on that part of life from being homeschooled. It was hard to miss people if you didn't see them often.

The door to the dorm room opened and closed quickly. Alex decided she wasn't going to pull the covers down. Maybe Jollies would leave her alone if she thought Alex was asleep. The pixie probably had other things to do than try to cheer Alex up anyway.

Alex was wrong. Her blanket was ripped away from her. She curled into the fetal position and shivered from the sudden cold.

Jollies flew to Alex's face and smiled brightly. "Up and at 'em!" she shouted. "You'll miss breakfast again if we don't move. Jeez, you really can sleep, you know that? I've never met anyone who can sleep as much as you."

Alex squinted and rubbed her eyes until Jollies came into focus. The pixie was bright, even brighter in the morning light. "What can I say? I'm very good at sleeping."

Jollies brightened even more as she zipped around Alex's head. "I know you're pretty committed to moping around in the morning, and I don't want to burst your bubble but..." She pointed at her eyes and then Alex's.

Alex didn't know what Jollies was miming at first, but then it clicked. She was looking at Jollies without her blindfold on, and without Manny anywhere near her. She was using her own eyes. "Holy cow!" Alex exclaimed.

That must have been what the slight headache was when she woke up. She hadn't even noticed she wasn't wearing her blindfold.

Jollies clapped her hands in excitement as she zipped around. "All right, if that's the case, I've got something you have to see with your own two eyes," Jollies exclaimed as she flew down and grabbed Alex's finger, yanking her out of bed.

Alex practically fell to the floor. She couldn't believe how strong Jollies was sometimes.

The pixie shoved Alex out of the room. "Come on! They're serving drow food. Yummy, yummy, yummy!"

In the hall, Alex turned and glared at Jollies. "What's drow food?" Alex asked.

Jollies smiled wide, and her color shifted to a deep purple. "Mostly snails and moss," Jollies answered. "Just kidding. Not about the snails and moss. About them serving it. They're not serving drow food. Just thought if I said that you'd move faster because of your interest in...you know. Now come on."

Jollies flew over to a poster of a large, white man with a golden beard on the wall just outside their door. He was extremely muscular and had beautiful eyes and a smile. Alex thought he was kinda cute.

Alex took a closer look at the poster. "Oh, yeah. He's cute, I guess," she said as she shrugged.

Jollies' color changed to dull blue. "I thought you'd be more excited."

"Uh, who is it?"

"What? You don't know? I was trying to make this place more human-friendly. Don't human girls like Chris Hemsworth?"

Alex laughed so hard her ribs hurt. "Jollies, I was blind for my entire life," she said. "I have no idea what Chris Hemsworth looks like."

Brath and Gill stepped out of their room. Alex hadn't realized it was directly across from her and Jollies'. Gill stopped to look at the poster and nodded. "Thor, huh?" Gill said softly. "I think Loki's cooler. The whole trickster god thing is pretty sweet."

Those were the first meaningful words Gill had spoken to Alex. She hadn't heard his voice before. It was extremely soft, and far too deep for someone his age. Her knees started to buckle.

Brath pushed his way forward to see the poster. "*Psh.* Some tough-looking human?" Brath croaked. "I should have assumed that a human would have such stupid taste. Why not a real hero like Gromnor the Gruesome or Aberdeen the Aberrant?"

Alex crossed her arms and leaned against the poster. "Screw you. I think he's hot," she spat. "He can kick ass and looks good doing it."

Brath scoffed loudly and fluffed his beard before he walked away. He looked over his shoulder at Gill. "Hey, are you coming?"

Gill nodded and turned his attention to Alex. "Catch you around," he said as he walked off.

Alex watched him join Brath as Jollies took a seat on her shoulder. "I bet I know who you want a poster of," she teased.

Alex's eyes shot daggers at the pixie. "We are not at that level of joking yet!" she exclaimed.

"We're roommates and breakfast buddies! We *are* on that level. And why do you want to get rid of the poster? I was just trying to help you feel at home. I didn't want to do anything to make anyone tease you more."

"No, leave it up. It's like a middle finger to Brath. He's probably just jealous that he's not that tall and buff."

Jollies' color shifted to white. "Middle finger?"

Alex gave Jollies the finger. "It's a human thing. It's a sign of disrespect."

"Oh, all right. Yeah, let's give Brath the middle finger, then!"

Jollies and Alex both flipped Brath off behind his back before they broke into giggles and went back to their room to get ready for the day.

CHAPTER SEVEN

Alex walked through the mess hall wearing her blindfold again, carrying the plate of food Jollies had brought her. She followed the pixie, who was leading her to a table full of her friends. Alex hadn't gotten a chance to meet any of them the day before, but honestly, there were so many, she doubted she would have remembered their names anyway.

The plate of food Alex held made no sense to her whatsoever. There was something yellow that looked like it could have been meat and then a pile of black mush that sizzled as if it were on fire. To top it all off, there was something that looked suspiciously like cheesecake.

None of it smelled appetizing. The pile of black mush smelled a lot like sulfur.

Alex took a seat next to where Jollies sat, if you could call it sitting. Pixies didn't really sit down and eat. They placed their plates on the table and gather together in a swarm, dipping down randomly to grab a morsel.

Alex tried to keep up with their conversation, but as she had noticed the day before, it was nearly impossible. The pixies spoke English, but they all seemed to talk at the same time and far too fast for Alex to catch what was being said.

That didn't bother Alex. She'd wanted to spend the morning alone with her thoughts anyway. This way, it wouldn't look like Alex was intentionally trying to spite her roommate. Besides, Jollies didn't seem to notice. It was the best of both worlds.

Alex replayed the look Gill had given her earlier by her room. It was nothing like how he or the rest of the cadets had looked at her before. There was something soft in his glance, almost as if he were curious.

Curious. She could handle that. She was curious about him as well. He didn't seem like the kind of guy who would hang out with Brath. He acted too soft and too artistic. All Alex could pick up from Brath was that he was a raging jerk.

Alex poked at her pile of black mush. *Well, I'm here to try new things,* she thought before tasting the mush. The flavor was overwhelming. It was like medium-rare steak and mashed potatoes at the same time.

Putting her spoon down, she eyed the mush, then she took a bite of the yellow piece of meat. It was sweet, almost as sweet as candy, and chewy like taffy. Then the sweetness was replaced by an almost salty taste.

Last, Alex took a bite of what looked like cheesecake. Surprisingly, the cheesecake tasted just like cheesecake.

All in all, Alex could say she *really* liked drow food.

As she dug into the strange new food, Brath and Gill walked past her table. Brath stopped, stared at what Alex was eating, and nudged Gill. "Check it out," Brath teased. "Guess the human finally got sick of being one and wants to try being a drow."

Gill looked at Alex, who had her mouth full of the mush. "Or perhaps she just appreciates the refined culinary skills of my people," Gill said drolly.

Brath put his plate on Alex's table and sat down. Gill sat next to him.

Alex took a deep breath and contemplated getting up and leaving, but she knew better. Brath was going to continue challenging her until she beat him. Running would just postpone the inevitable. Besides, Alex was tired of running. She was going to stand her ground.

Brath took a savage bite of a leg of mutton. "So, how long do you think it's going to take you to find your way into the Dark One's dungeons?" the gnome asked.

Alex didn't look up from her food as she replied, "Probably twice as long as it's going to take you, and that's if he doesn't end up stepping on you accidentally."

The pixies stopped talking as the byplay between Brath and Alex caught their attention. Jollies left the swarm and landed on Alex's hand.

Brath laughed viciously. "You talk a big game for someone who couldn't even finish the race in a reasonable amount of time," Brath shot back. "From what I heard, you had the worst time of any cadet in the history of the academy. Slowest dragonrider ever. That's if you even make the cut."

Alex casually took a bite of the meat. "Better than the smelliest dragonrider," she retorted. "Or is that gaseous cloud of body odor a gnome thing? I've been wanting to ask, because, to be frank, you're the only gnome I've met who smells like the backside of a troll."

The pixies erupted into gales of laughter and their bodies shimmered from bright red to pink. Jollies giggled. Alex tried to pretend none of this was affecting her. Her heart was racing, though.

Brath's face reddened behind his white beard. "You can talk as much trash as you want. I'm still going to knock you on your ass at the joust!" he shouted as he slammed his fist on the table.

Alex's face must have betrayed her surprise because Brath burst out laughing and pointed a snide finger at her. "Look at you! You don't even know there's a joust today. You probably don't even know what a joust is."

"I don't need to know what it is to beat you at it!" Alex shouted back.

The rest of the mess hall was starting to pay attention to their fight. Gill just ate quietly at Brath's side as if he couldn't hear either of them.

Brath climbed onto the table so he was at eye level with Alex. "Doesn't matter what you *think* you're going to do," he said. "I'm not letting a lazy human who thinks she's better than everyone waltz in here and become a dragonrider."

Jollies flew between them. "Hey, come on, Brath," she said. "Do you really want to be the guy who's known for picking on the blind girl?"

Alex's pride flashed red-hot. She stood and gently pushed Jollies out of the way so she could face Brath. "I'm not 'the blind girl' or 'the human,'" Alex shouted. "I'm Alex Bound, and I'm the one who's going to massacre you at the joust today."

The door of the mess hall burst open, and all the cadets jumped.

Fier had come in. She was wearing her armor and she did not look pleased. "What the hell are you cadets still doing in here?" she shouted. "Don't you know better than to ride on a full stomach?"

Fier hung her head as she shook it. "Go get suited up! I want you all on the training field in a half-hour. *GET MOVING!*"

63

CHAPTER EIGHT

The cadets gathered in the same field as the day before. It had changed dramatically, though. Bleachers had been set up, and crystal walls created an arena.

Between the bleachers was a grandstand where the instructors sat. There were two dragonriders Alex didn't recognize. She looked for Jollies in the crowd to ask if she knew who they were.

Instructions were blaring over a loudspeaker, explaining how the joust was going to work. Multiple matches were going to run simultaneously. The winner of each match went on to the next round.

Where these jousts differed from basic tournaments was that each player was going to be scored on technique by the two judges. These scores would be compared across all cadets, and that was how the winner would be chosen.

Fier stood on the grandstand with the other instructors and raised her hands to silence the chatty cadets. "The rules are simple," she explained. "You all know how a joust works. Whoever knocks the other player off their dragon wins.

That's about the only rule we got. And don't worry, we'll make sure you don't die, so don't hold back."

Alex pushed her way through the crowd that was slowly starting to split up and form into their cadet year groups. She found Jollies with the rest of the first years. "Hey, Jollies. Who are those other two riders?"

Jollies' wings flashed a bright yellow as she flew in a circle. "Oh, right, you don't know them, do you?" the pixie asked. She pulled down her HUD and projected a holographic image of one of the riders.

He was a grizzled, middle-aged human. A scar ran down the side of his face, and his eyes looked as if they had seen horrors. "This is Roy," Jollies explained. "He's one of the most decorated Mech-riders ever. He fights in this weird dragon mech thing. You'll have to see it to believe it. He's been in more battles than any other rider."

Jollies flipped to the next rider, a lanky, sturdy-looking woodland elf. His ears had a regal point to them, and he was not smiling. "And that's Toppinir. He's another veteran. Some people think he's the best dragonrider ever. Like, the greatest in history."

Jollies shut down her HUD as the two of them made their way to the bleachers. "They sometimes pick squires from the winners of the tournaments," Jollies said, "but that hasn't happened in a long time. I think Toppinir's last squire died in battle almost a decade ago."

The first joust got underway. Two cadets Alex hadn't seen before took the field. On the opposite side, two of the older cadets flew into the air.

The joust took place too high in the air for Alex to see, so she politely made small talk with a cadet next to her who was raving about how much she wanted to meet Roy. Jollies was surprisingly quiet while she watched the match.

One of the cadets was knocked off his dragon, and he

yelped loudly as he plummeted toward the ground. Suddenly, a web-like net popped into existence, and the cadet bounced up and down before disappearing. He reappeared at the far end of the bleachers in an area aptly titled the Loser's Box.

Alex turned to Jollies and said, "They don't have to be so mean about it."

Jollies giggled and nodded in agreement. "I feel like some of the professors really enjoy being jerks to us," she admitted.

Two more matches took place, and Alex lamented her inability to see what was going on. She thought about using Chine's eyes if he would let her but thought better of it. Instead, she concentrated on using her own eyes and ignoring Manny's view. Her vision was still very limited and overwhelming, but she was adjusting slowly. She needed to practice to get used to her gift.

Fier's voice rang over the loudspeaker. "Next up, Brath and Jollies!" she shouted.

Jollies squeaked loudly when she heard her name and turned to Alex. "Wish me luck," she squealed before flying off.

On the other side of the bleachers, Brath stood and made his way to the field.

Jollies and Brath raised their dragon anchors into the air, and their dragons rocketed toward them. They chose lances from the weapons rack and took off.

Alex took a deep breath and squinted, and when she focused her right eye, she could see Jollies and Brath crystal-clear.

The two cadets had already started their fight. Jollies was whizzing past Brath as his dragon spewed fire everywhere in complete and utter disregard for safety. Luckily, Jollies was too fast to be hit.

Jollies leapt from her dragon and flew straight for Brath's head. Her lance hit him in the forehead, knocking him backward. His dragon, Furi, lunged upward as the rider lost his balance.

Amber, Jollies' dragon, swept under the pixie and scooped her up.

Alex was impressed with Jollies' tactics. Brath and Furi were too large for her to overpower, so splitting up with Amber and trying to knock both Brath and Furi off balance made the most sense.

Jollies went for Brath from behind this time. She leaped off her dragon again, landed on Furi's back, ran up to Brath, and swooped his legs out from under him. When Brath hit his dragon's back, Jollies' lance magically extended, unseating him.

He fell through the air but managed to hold onto his lance. He raised his dragon anchor and Furi turned in midair and came shooting toward him. He slipped under Brath to save his rider from falling.

Jollies wasn't ready to back off. After getting back on Amber, she flew toward Brath as fast as she could, electricity crackling off her dragon's scales.

Brath turned with his lance in his free hand, and it extended and flattened into the shape of a flyswatter. He smashed the lance against Jollies' dragon, sending the pixie flying through the air.

Furi let out a condensed fireball that hit Amber in the chest, and the electric dragon fell toward the ground.

Brath raised the fly-swatting lance again and landed his final blow, and Jollies' little pixie body crumpled. She followed her dragon toward the ground.

The invisible magic web popped up again and caught both rider and dragon, then it sent Jollies to the Loser's Box and Amber to who knew where.

Alex stood so she could meet Jollies in the box, but Fier's

voice over the loudspeaker stopped her. "Alex Bound and Gill Lowborn. Meet on the field."

Fear rose in Alex, but she pushed it down. This wasn't the time for that; she could be afraid later. Right now, she had to prove herself. She jogged down to the field to meet Gill, who was calmly making his way over.

The two stood facing each other. Gill didn't look concerned when he leaned over and asked, "Aren't you taking Manny with you?"

Alex shook her head. She'd thought this over. Manny was what had held her back last time. She could see well enough through the blindfold, something only Jollies knew, and she planned to use that to her advantage.

Fier's voice came from the speaker again. "Begin!"

Both riders grabbed lances and raised their dragon anchors to the sky, but Alex turned and ran away from Gill. She was still holding her anchor high but pointing it ahead of her.

Chine slammed to the ground a few feet in front of her. She leaped onto him, turned, and aimed her lance at Gill. She wasn't sure how the magic worked, but she envisioned her lance stretching as far as it could.

The lance responded to her psychic command and went flying toward Gill, whose eyes widened in surprise. He jumped out of the way as Timber landed next to him.

Alex retracted her lance and pulled back on her anchor, sending Chine soaring into the air. *Well, that was an interesting tactic*, the dragon mused. *A little aggressive, wouldn't you say?*

It'll knock him off-balance, she replied. *He'll be thinking the entire time, 'How did a blind girl do that?' Half of any fight is mental.*

Chine laughed loudly in her head as he turned in the air to face Gill. *I like this part of you, Dustling. You have a warrior deep within you.*

Alex and Gill stared at each other across the skies. Alex's heart was fluttering; she wished she could better see Gill's black eyes, but this wasn't the time for that. She could see the outline of him and his dragon, and that was all she needed. Her crush could wait until later.

Gill made the first move. He flew at Alex full-speed, which caught her off-guard. She had assumed the drow would be much more calculating in his strategy. He seemed like such a passive person.

Alex pulled Chine to the left, narrowly avoiding Gill, who hadn't even bothered to raise his lance. He must have just been planning to have Timber tackle Chine. *Why would he do that?* Alex thought. *He could be knocked off as well.*

Gill wasted no time. He turned instantly and went for another attack. Alex hardly had a moment to recover and narrowly missed being knocked to the ground.

Timber looked over his shoulder, opened his mouth, and sent a concussive force through the air that hit Alex square in the chest.

The force of the blast almost knocked her off Chine. Her chest heaved in pain, and she doubled over. She hadn't been prepared for Gill to attack her straight on. Also, she couldn't see the attack. She tried to remember what she'd read about earth dragons the day before.

All of a sudden, her late-night reading came back to her. *Chine!* she said. *I need you to watch for Timber's invisible attacks. I can't see them. I can only see outlines. Can you dodge them on your own?*

Her opponents were flying toward her again. She heard the blast charging in Timber's throat, but she couldn't tell where it was going to come from. *Easily.* Chine chuckled as he turned to the right and dipped so the blast went past him.

Alex was about to congratulate him when Gill's lance came shooting toward her. She wasn't able to move in time, and it hit her shoulder. She almost lost balance, but then she gripped more tightly, strengthening her anchor to Chine. As she pulled right and let the dragon roll in midair, hoping she wouldn't fall while the dragon was upside-down.

The gamble worked. Alex didn't need to be right-side-up anyway, and now she had a plan. *Chine, you can briefly turn invisible, right?*

For a few seconds. Maybe a minute.

All right. On my signal, use your invisibility.

Alex didn't bother turning him upright. Instead, she flew under Gill and stomped on Chine's back as the signal to camouflage himself.

Chine shimmered out of sight, and Alex waited for Gill to take the bait. "Tell me when his lance hits you," she commanded.

Alex heard the lance hit Chine's stomach as the dragon said, "He's made contact. Alex released her dragon anchor as she held onto Chine's back, then she scrambled up his side as fast as she could until she got to his stomach.

Alex knew invisibility only applied to the person who could turn invisible. When her dragon popped out of sight, all Gill would see was Alex, a defenseless target. She banked on him attacking before thinking the odd sight through.

Alex reached out and grabbed Gill's lance, pulling hard.

Out of reflex, Gill leaned back and called his lance back, which was just what Alex was waiting for. She held as tightly as she could to the lance as it withdrew back to Gill.

She stretched out her lance and focused, launching it at Gill as his was returning to its normal length.

It hit Gill in the chest, and he lost his grip on his own and went flying through the air. Alex attached her dragon anchor to Timber and pulled as hard as she could, fighting with Timber for control. It was just enough.

Timber pulled hard to the left as his rider went flying off

the dragon's right side. Once she heard Gill hit the net, she detached from Timber and leapt off as she called to Chine, *Please don't let me fall!*

The dragon swooped under Alex, and she landed on his back. *I believed you had a warrior in you. I didn't realize she was a madwoman.*

Chine and Alex touched down to the cheers of the other cadets. Alex rushed over to the Loser's Box while Chine took off.

Jollies was waiting for Alex and exclaimed, "That was amazing!"

Gill walked up behind Alex and bowed. "It really was. You use…very unorthodox tactics."

Alex blushed and waved away Gill's compliment. "Let me take a seat with you guys."

The three of them watched the next few matches, Alex occasionally pulling up her blindfold on one eye, practicing being able to see for longer periods of time. Finally, Fier called her name again. "Alex Bound and Brath Gimbel to the field."

Alex leaped out of her seat. "Wish me luck," she said before turning to Manny. "Come on. Let's go."

Manny jumped at Alex's voice. "Wait, me? You did so well on your own."

"Nope, you're not getting out of this. I need you." She had a plan that needed Manny's sight to pull off. In fact, it needed more than just his sight. She'd need to use all her eyes.

Brath was already waiting for Alex on the field. He didn't bother looking at her, just raised his dragon anchor before Fier said anything. Within a few seconds, Furi hit the ground behind him, radiating smoke and heat.

Alex raised her own and Chine promptly landed behind her, ether smoke seeping from his nostrils. Alex leaped onto him, and neither she nor Brath waited for Fier to declare the fight had begun.

The dragons rose higher than any of the other drag-onriders had, and the riders glared at each other. "All right, human, time to learn your place!" the gnome shouted.

Furi shot a blast of fire at Chine as he and Brath flew around, trying to flank Alex. Brath pointed his lance, and it went flying toward her.

She pulled back on Chine, doing a barrel roll that set Manny screaming. The dragon shot ether fire, canceling out Furi's blast.

Furi screamed in rage and bolted toward Chine, and the two dragons collided. Furi's claws raked across Chine's chest.

As the dragons fought, Brath pulled off his cloak, then ran up Furi's head, leaped through the air, and tossed his cloak on Manny.

The cloth wrapped around Manny as if it were alive. Alex turned and tried to pull the coat off Manny but couldn't. It must have been magic.

Brath ran back to his spot on Furi's back. "Gotcha!" he shouted. "What's a dragonrider without her eyes?"

Alex reached out to Chine. *Hey, can you keep everything steady?* she asked. *Don't let go of Furi, but give us a big show, all right? Lots of roaring and fire.*

Chine's voice boomed in Alex's head. *I can do that,* he said as he produced another jet of black ether fire.

Alex stood up, grabbed her blindfold, and pulled it off. The light was dazzling at first, but she closed her eyes to concentrate before opening them again. Now she saw the world through her own eyes.

Everything was clear. She could see each scale on Furi's and Chine's bodies. She could tell how far away Brath was and see the confusion in his eyes. He'd expected her to use Manny's vision.

He had underestimated her, and he was going to pay for that mistake.

Don't let go of Furi, all right? she requested of her dragon.

Alex ran down Chine's back, raised her lance, and jumped, stretching the wood out like a pole. Vaulting over the dragons' heads, she passed through the chaos of fire and kicked Brath square in the chest.

Brath went flying, but Alex didn't stop there. She punched him off the big dragon, then leapt off Furi, aimed her lance at Brath, and concentrated. The weapon struck Brath's chest, and he fell faster.

The invisible net popped out beneath him, and he disappeared as soon as he hit it.

Alex's lance caught the net and stopped her from falling. She swayed back and forth on the pole until Chine sped down to catch her. The net disappeared and Chine landed, then Alex jumped off his back, leaving Manny to fend for himself. She was greeted by the roars of the crowd of cadets. He finally pried the cloak off his head and floated disgustedly off the field.

Fier's excited voice rose over the crowd. "And after an insane gamble, Alex Bound is the winner of the first-year cadets jousting competition!" she shouted.

Roy and Toppinir, who were sitting at Fier's side, rose as well. They lifted their hands to quiet the crowd. Alex turned to face them, not knowing what else to do since she was still in the middle of the field.

Toppinir stepped forward, his hands still extended. "We have the collected points of all champions." He paused, letting the tension build. "And the champion of today's jousts is Alex Bound, with fifteen thousand and thirty-five points for technique, skill, and unrivaled showmanship!"

The first-year cadets broke into cheers as they tackled Alex, who had quickly wrapped her blindfold back around her head. Jollies was buzzing in Alex's ears. "Did you hear that, Alex? You won!"

Toppinir's voice came over the loudspeaker again as he leaned over and spoke with Roy. "I haven't seen a match like that in years," he whispered, despite it being loudly broadcast. "We should keep an eye on that Bound cadet."

Jollies grabbed Alex's cheeks. "By the gods, you did it!"

Alex laughed as she pried the pixie's hands off. "Yeah. Yeah, I did." She laughed. "I might not become a squire, but that kind of shout-out has to count for something, right?"

"You bet it does!"

Alex let herself get lost in the cheers of the crowd. She'd done it; this was her victory, and no one could take it away from her.

CHAPTER NINE

The pixies and the other new cadets brought Alex into the mess hall atop their shoulders. They had broken into a chant in a language Alex didn't recognize. She assumed it was Dwarfish, from what she'd heard in *Middang3ard*.

The mess hall was filled with the sounds of victory. The tables were decorated with the colors of the first-year cadets, and bottles of pixie mead had been placed on each. Pixies couldn't drink alcohol, so the beverage was often provided to the underage cadets.

Alex was taken to the largest table in the mess hall, which was covered with plate upon plate of decadent-looking meats and desserts. The cadets tried to get her to take the seat at the head of the table, but she opted out, instead choosing to sit toward the middle.

Jollies took a sip from one of the pixie-sized cups as she flew toward Alex. "That was amazing, Alex," she gushed. "I didn't know you could ride like that. Hell, I didn't know *any* first years could ride like that!"

Alex laughed and tried not to let the praise go to her head, which was extremely difficult since this was the first good dragonriding-related thing she'd heard about herself. "Eh, it wasn't anything," she said. "I'm not going to say I just got lucky, but there was some luck in there."

The excitement from the joust hadn't worn off. The rest of the cadets were all talking excitedly among themselves, going over each match play by play.

Alex could feel the change in the room and in the way others were looking at her now. It felt good not to be seen as some kind of disabled charity case. It felt even better to shove Brath's stupid face in his failure.

Brath and Gill were sitting together across the mess hall. The gnome was stewing over his pixie mead, staring into the cup as if he could arrive at some understanding by contemplating the liquid within. Gill was talking quietly with a light elf who was sitting next to him.

Alex didn't realize she had been staring at Gill for some time. Even with her blindfold on, she could see him nearly as clearly as if she weren't wearing it. It helped that Manny was on the other side of the room, snacking as usual. He had apparently recovered from their wild flight. Alex was looking forward to not relying so heavily on the Beholder's assistance.

Suddenly, Brath slammed down his cup. The table he was sitting at went silent as he stood and stalked over to Alex. "How'd you do it, human?" Brath asked. "You must have cheated!"

For a second, Alex worried that Brath had heard the brief conversation she'd had with Chine, but it wouldn't have mattered even if he had. She'd told her dragon she wanted to play it straight. No tricks. She wanted to win on her own merits.

Alex leaned back in her seat, feeling more like her old self —the confident dragonrider who had impressed all of

Middang3ard VR. "No such thing happened," Alex replied, trying not to sound like she was gloating. "I won fair and square. Don't be such a sore loser."

"I want a rematch. I'm not losing to a stinkin' human."

"You already lost to a human. A rematch will just mean you get to lose again. Can your pride handle that?"

Brath didn't say anything, just glared at Alex. "What's your problem with me anyway?" she asked. "Why does a blind human being a dragonrider affect you in any way? It's not like there are a limited number of cadets who can make it through."

"Because I don't want my ass getting scorched because some human can't keep up. That's how it's been with all of you. When the gnomish and dwarfish realms asked for help, your people did nothing. You just sat on the sidelines and watched our worlds disappear. The only reason you're here is that you humans suddenly realized you were in danger too."

Alex could see the pain in Brath's eyes. He looked close to tears. For the first time, she understood how much he was hurting. "Brath, I didn't have any control over that," she told him softly. "I only just found out about the war, and as soon as I did, I decided to come. I wouldn't—"

"I don't care!" he shouted.

The two stared at each other as the rest of the cadets watched.

The door to the mess hall exploded open as the second-year cadets burst into the room. "Where's the chick who won?" one of the elvish cadets shouted.

The first-year cadets all pointed at Alex.

The second-year cadets stormed to her table and surrounded it. The elf who had shouted upon entering the mess hall stood in front of Alex. "How in the gods' names did you pull that off?" he asked. "Aren't you supposed to be blind?"

Alex pointed at her blindfold. "Formerly blind, but I'm still working on it," she coyly replied. "So, are all dragonrider cadets whiny sore losers?"

The elf flipped Alex's plate over, and some of the food hit Jollies in the face. "There's no way a blind first-year beat all of us second-years without cheating," the elf exclaimed.

Alex stood and leaned over the table. "If you want, us first-years could come give you lessons," she countered. "I'm pretty sure Jollies and Gill could show you a few things. Even Brath could; he still beat all you second-years."

Brath looked at Alex, obviously surprised she had included him in the list.

The elf leaned forward, nearly nose to nose with Alex. "Or we could just wipe the floor with you all right now," he threatened.

Jollies zipped over to the elf, wiped the food off her face and smeared it across his. "How about we end it right now?" Jollies shouted before flying down, picking up a whole plate of food, and shoving it in the elf's face.

The elf stepped back and wiped the mashed potatoes off. His eyes were red with anger.

Jollies grabbed another handful of food and tossed it at him, shouting, "*Food fight!*" before flying away, grabbing Alex by the shoulder, and pulling her under the table.

Gill and Brath followed them as the mess hall exploded into a battlefield of edible projectiles, liquids as well.

Alex and the other three crawled farther beneath the table as they tried to avoid being hit by the artillery.

Jollies turned to Alex and Brath, grabbing each of them by their collars, and forced them to look at each other in the eye. "Okay, I know you guys have issues with each other," the pixie said. "But right now, we have more important things to deal with. Do you want to get wrecked by those second-years?"

Alex and Brath gazed at each other. She sure did not want to look like something a sick second-year had thrown up. "All right, I get it," she said. She extended her hand to the gnome. "Truce?"

Brath glared at Alex, his eyes still full of hate. "Just because there's a food fight, it doesn't mean your people didn't leave us to die," he growled.

"Yeah, you're right, but even if my people didn't help yours, it doesn't mean I'm not here to help you. I'm right here in front of you, aren't I? That means I'm here to fight the Dark One, just like you, and I'll protect anyone who needs it."

Brath looked at Gill, who nodded silently. "Fine," Brath conceded. "Truce."

Gill smiled, the first time Alex had seen him do so, and reached up to the table. He felt around, brought a handful of the black mush down, and took a quick bite. "Are you guys ready to show the second-years that seniority doesn't mean squat?" he asked.

Jollies, Alex, and Brath nodded in agreement. "All right," Alex said. "Let's show 'em why the first-year cadets destroyed the second-years in the joust."

Alex rolled out from under the table and shouted, "For the glory of the first-years! May we live in legend!"

Alex tossed a handful of peas at the closest person, only to get a face full of pink and blue cake thrown hard enough to knock her off her feet. Jollies and the rest of them slid out from under the table and grabbed whatever they could before chucking it.

Gill and Brath knelt and helped Alex to her feet. The gnome grabbed Alex's blindfold, which had been knocked off, wiped it clean, and handed it to Gill, who promptly wrapped it around her head.

The mess hall was quickly earning its name. Food was flying from every direction, and it was impossible to see which year was attacking whom. Some of the dwarves had decided to sit the fight out and were casually enjoying lunch in the midst of the pandemonium.

Manny was content to nonchalantly float through the mess hall, licking up anything he came across.

Alex stood back to back with Brath, flinging whatever they could get their hands on, whether it was coming from the tables or they were pulling it off their clothes.

A gnome came running up to Alex, screaming loudly. Brath stepped to the side, pushed Alex out of the way, and decked the gnome with a heavy handful of elvish peas.

Alex smiled at Brath. "Hey, thanks!"

Brath shrugged. "Don't mention it."

Suddenly, a shrill, ear-piercing noise broke through the chaos. Everyone stopped as the door to the mess hall was flung open. Fier, Professor Choice, and Tribble all ran in.

Fier, eyes wide with fury, surveyed the situation. "What in the nine realms is going on here?" she shouted. "Oh, by the gods, there's no time! Every student to your rooms! *NOW!*"

The students looked at each other for a moment before Fier shouted again for them to get moving. There was no time to ask questions. The cadets funneled out of the mess hall as the teachers hurried them along.

What is going on? Alex thought.

CHAPTER TEN

As the cadets rushed toward their rooms, Alex tried her best to figure out what was going on. The instructors didn't seem to have any time to explain. They weren't even the ones herding the students to the rooms; that responsibility had been left to a handful of the scientists.

Alex, Jollies, and Manny had almost reached her room when she heard a violent explosion. It was impossible to tell how far away it was, but it sounded as if a bomb had gone off in the Nest.

Another explosion went off, this time much closer. The entire hallway shook, and specks of crystal fell from the ceiling. *Are we being attacked?* Alex thought as she looked around.

Adrenaline pumped through her body. She'd never been in an actual fight, let alone something on this scale. The closest she'd gotten was the food fight she had just participated in.

She turned to Jollies, who was flying behind them. "What's going on?"

Jollies flew higher to get a better look at the situation,

then zipped back down to Alex and said, "I have no idea. I can't see anything."

Gill, who was at their side, nonchalantly said, "It sounds like an attack."

"How? Isn't the Wasp's Nest magically hidden from everyone?"

Gill nodded, his face grim and resolute. "Any spell can be broken if you hit it hard enough," he replied. "Maybe someone knows what they're doing?"

Brath opened his door and stepped inside, leaving it open for Gill, who quickly followed. Gill waited for a moment and then called to Alex and Jollies, "You guys should stay in here. It'd be safer for us to be together."

Jollies zipped into the room without asking any questions. Alex and Manny followed, and Gill shut the door quietly, then walked to a corner, sat down, and folded his legs.

The boys' room had an entirely different personality than Jollies' and Alex's. To begin with, it was covered in flowers and plants Alex had never seen before. There was an altar to some god in the corner next to Gill. The other side of the room was covered in rugby posters and holographic statues of gnomes, so it was clearly Brath's side.

Brath climbed onto his bed and opened his book. "Make yourselves comfortable," he said with only the slightest hint of disgust in his voice.

Alex sat down across from Gill, still taking the room in. "Can we be attacked so easily?" she asked.

Gill stretched his arms as he re-crossed his legs. "Definitely," he said softly. "We are at war. It isn't uncommon for the Dark One to attack training grounds. Easiest way to make sure no one can get new recruits or backup."

Jollies was still flying around, her colors shifting as if she were a buzzing rainbow. "Yeah, it happens all the time," she agreed. "Just a few months ago, the pixie infantry's training grounds were attacked. Completely wiped out. It could happen to anyone."

Alex reached toward Jollies, sensing how distraught she was. "Hey, come here," she suggested.

Jollies stopped in midair and flew to Alex, landed on her chest, and scooted close to her ear. Alex could hear the pixie's teeth chattering. In an attempt to take Jollies' mind— and her own—off what was happening, Alex pointed to the holographs near Brath's bed. "Hey, what are those?"

Brath's eyes rose above the pages of his book. "Those?" he repeated. "That's my family. It's all I have left of them. They were in the dwarfish realm when it was taken over. That's why I'm here. It was either this or an orphanage. I figured I couldn't kill the Dark One from an orphanage."

Alex was shocked by Brath's frankness. She knew there was a war on an intellectual level since that was the reason she was here, but she hadn't understood how it had affected those she was training with. She wanted to kick herself for being so naïve.

"I'm sorry," she finally said.

Brath returned to his book. "The Dark One will be too," he muttered.

Alex turned her attention back to Gill, who had his HUD visor on. "What are you doing?" she asked.

Gill pulled the visor up for a second, smiling in a way that made his sharp incisors gleam. "Something I'm not supposed to be," he said. "Pull up your HUDs and I'll patch you through."

Jollies and Alex opened their HUDs, and security camera footage started to play. Alex could see the crystal corridors of the Wasp's Nest. "What is this?" she asked.

Gill explained, "I hacked into the system. Check this out."

The camera angle changed. Alex saw a group of ten orcs

hacking at one of the crystal doors. When the angle changed again, different orcs set explosives before running away. "Crap, I guess we *are* being attacked," she murmured.

The angle changed again. A group of orcs was running down the hall and screaming with their swords raised. "Wait," Gill whispered. "Is that a human poster? Zoom in."

The camera zoomed in—it was the poster of Chris Hemsworth as Thor. The orcs stopped in front of it, confused, entranced, or both.

"Oh, no!" Alex exclaimed. "They're right outside."

Alex and the Boundless face a new challenge. The Dark One has done the impossible and infiltrated the Nest. Can they defend it? Find out in *Nest Under Siege*!

At the time of this publication, New Years wasn't too long ago. And one of the most common things that's comes up with New Years are resolutions... But I no longer do them. I've found that resolutions are usually things I can't do. Give up chocolate, exercise more, stop leaving my underwear all over the house (wait... I would never do that... *Looks around guiltily.*)

That's why I've traded New Years' Resolutions for themes.

In 2018, my theme was to live outside my comfort zone. To symbolize that, I started to wear two bright and mismatching socks every day. You see, when I was a kid, I was briefly bullied because I didn't wear name-brand jeans. I don't want to blow it out of proportion. It lasted a few months, and the kid leading the charge is most likely in jail now (so in the long run, I win). But it was still a sore point in my childhood and something that lingered. So wearing mismatching socks did make me uncomfortable—the operative word: *did...*

I've been wearing them for two years and have gotten over that phobia.

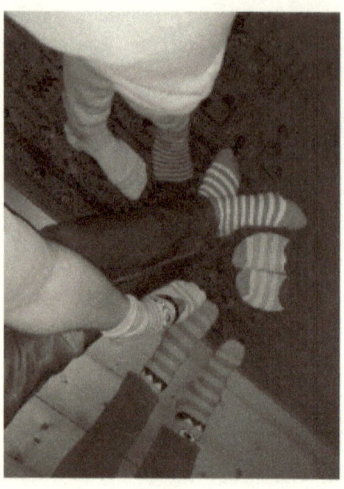

In 2019, my theme was my year of YES. One of my mentors (perhaps you've heard of her: Martha Carr) told me to say YES to everything. At first, I thought she was insane (I also thought about that Jim Carrey movie). But seeing her success and realizing that she probably knew some things I didn't, I began saying YES to *almost* everything.

Because of YES, I helped organize 20Books Edinburgh. It was a hell of a lot of work and stress, but in the end it was worth it. Whereas I can't say loved every minute of it, I did love that I got be part of bringing together so many talented people. (*PLUS I met all of the GoneGod World authors there.*)

It also saw me doing more traveling than I have ever done in one single year. Mostly conferences and author events (with one three-day trip to Austin for an author gathering). It was an exhausting year, but so, so worth it.

The results were incredible. I learned so much… Saying YES literally supercharged my year.

Now 2020 is here and it's time for a new theme. This year is CONSISTENCY. I will endeavor to be consistent in everything I do. That means writing, eating healthy, family time, doing the boring tasks that I hate but are good for me… And I'll be consistent in forgiving myself should I be inconsistent, too.

I'm looking forward to this theme. 2018 and 2019 really were supercharged years for me. 2020 will hopefully be the same.

What was your New Years' resolution or theme? I'd love to hear from you…

As always, you can find me in my FB Group: House of the GoneGod Damned! Or sign up to my NL, where I promise to consistently (but not annoyingly) email you :)

Cheers! Here's to one hell of a 2020!

Thank you for reading this story and checking in on us in the back!

I agree with Ramy's themes idea.

Last year, I had put a goal for our company to accomplish publishing four hundred (400) books. We didn't make it (we were between three and four hundred somewhere), but more than that, the goal I set wasn't the end goal. (*Editor's note: We published on the high side of 350*)

The end goal was to *"Test Ourselves."*

Meaning, I wanted to push our company so hard, we knew what we could accomplish and to grow our backlist, providing us a large group of stories for our fans to read. It was a "BAHG," which is short for Big Hairy Audacious Goal.

Otherwise known in the company as "**Are you f##king kidding me?**"

In 2018, where the theme was "Let's prepare for 2019 where we do 400 books," we built an infrastructure towards the goal of making that happen. We put on our thinking hats and sharpened our pencils to figure out how to get to 400.

What stories were we going to do? Who (exactly) were going to be doing it? How would we get 400 covers done? How many words of editing would we need to be able to accomplish?

(The answer is a metric sh##load.)

We went running through 2019 like a bunch of teenagers trying to catch free cash raining from the heavens. It was a lot of fun, but man oh man, was it dangerous!

Lynne: I edited between 800k and 1.2m words per month last year, as did my co-editor. Holy schnikes! No wonder we're tired! But we did learn a lot, mostly that we could not sustain that pace, so for me, see the theme below and substitute "the editing team" for "ourselves."

We broke (more) than a few things, but in the end, we survived. We are stronger, more capable, and more than that, we are wise beyond our years. *(Editor's Note. I'd say wiser. "Wise" just challenges us to come up with better, more creative errors.)*

How can I say that? Because wisdom comes with doing, and the more you do, the more wisdom you earn.

On average (a very odd word, but the best one I can use), a publishing company will put out up to twenty-four books a year.

Some, like Baen Books, do about seventy-two a year.

We published four to five times Baen Books' total and twelve times that of an average publishing company.

So, we acquired a LOT of wisdom, pushing the company and our creativity. Some of the wounds we suffered I'm sure will heal in 2020. Some won't.

So as we come into 2020, we have a new theme, and it is…

The Year of Unf##king ourselves.

How's THAT for a theme?

;-)

Ad Aeternitatem,

Michael Anderle

OTHER BOOKS BY THE AUTHORS

Other Middang3ard Books

Never Split The Party (01)
Late To the Party (02)
It's My Party (03)
Blue Hell And Alien Fire (04)

Death Of An Author: A Middang3ard Novella

Other Books by Ramy Vance

Mortality Bites Series
Keep Evolving Series
Fatebound Series

Other Books by Michael Anderle

For a complete list of books by Michael Anderle, please visit:

www.lmbpn.com/ma-books/

All LMBPN Audiobooks are Available at Audible.com and iTunes. To see all LMBPN audiobooks, including those written by Michael Anderle please visit:

www.lmbpn.com/audible

CONNECT WITH THE AUTHORS

Connect with Ramy

Join Ramy's Newsletter

Join Ramy's FB Group: House of the GoneGod Damned!

Connect with Michael Anderle and sign up for his email list here:

Website: http://lmbpn.com

Email List: http://lmbpn.com/email/

Facebook:
www.facebook.com/TheKurtherianGambitBooks

www.ingramcontent.com/pod-product-compliance
Lightning Source LLC
Chambersburg PA
CBHW050155110726
47898CB00008B/2813